The House At Roc Noir

Julia Laflin

The House At Roc Noir

Julia Laflin

Contents:

I The Arrival   7
II The Stay   20
III The Aftermath   91

A message from the author   108
Acknowledgements   109
About the author   110

I The Arrival

It was so unlike Nick to plan any kind of surprise, let alone a holiday, thought Alice. She was torn between a rush of love for him, for secretly planning her birthday celebration, and slight trepidation.

The idea was his and she was more than happy to seize on it. A big fuss over her fiftieth birthday, partying with friends and family, was not what she wanted. A trip away, just the two of them, then lunch in London with a couple of close girlfriends, would do fine. So she responded enthusiastically.

'A holiday would be lovely, darling. Just tell me what to pack.'

This break had come at a good time, Alice thought. Maybe the big birthday looming ahead of her was making her focus too much on ageing in all its unwelcome aspects. I need this holiday to realign myself, she decided. She was aware of feeling loss on many levels: her looks, her sense of purpose, her sense of control over her own life. It wouldn't do. Anxiety seemed to be taking hold of her more often these days. She dithered over the smallest decisions, shied away from risk and was apprehensive about the future. Nick had remarked recently on what he saw as a change in her behaviour in rather a negative fashion and it had hurt when he said it.

* * *

'Mum will love that!'

Nick had no trouble choosing their destination. It was a place he had always wanted to visit and now Cally, their twenty-three year old daughter, was helping him to vet accommodation online, a task complicated by Tabbicat, the family pet, tenacious in her attempts to pace the desk and block their view of the laptop screen.

The deserted bay of Marina du Roc Noir that Nick showed her would be perfect for Alice. It was better in every way than the built-up resorts she abhorred. Wild, natural seascapes were Alice's favourite thing and Cally agreed with Nick that her mother would not care, at that time of year, that the beach was stony.

'It'll be late April, so it's a spring break really. We can do a bit of exploring and have plenty of relaxing *al fresco* lunches but it won't really be hot enough for a sand and sunbathing type holiday.'

It was only when he opened the rudimentary website of the Relais de la Mer that Cally became less enthusiastic.

She looked at the photo gallery of the Relais displayed on the screen. The first picture showed an external view of a two-storey building the size of a large house, angled into the far left of a rocky bay. It was the only building right on the waterfront, apart from a romantic looking stone tower up the other end.

'Um...' Cally paused as if groping for the right words. 'It's not that it's ugly. It's just, well, a bit uninspiring.'

'Wait, before you pass judgement. I'll show you more.'

The next image was far more appealing. It featured the terrace that ran along the front of the Relais before spreading wide, effectively linking the building to the side sweep of cliff at the end of the bay. But the series of interior shots that followed displayed a handful of identical double rooms: plain, clean and characterless.

'It's a bit basic, isn't it?' When it came to holidays, Cally's aspirations tended towards boutique hotel rooms equipped with deep pile towelling robes and luxury toiletries. 'Isn't there anywhere else you can stay?' she asked.

'Not with this exceptional setting. There's nothing much else around. Only a set of *gîtes* up in the hills behind the bay, with a very distant view of the sea.'

'But those rooms are so dated.'

'Ignore the rooms. There's an apartment on the first floor beyond them. I'm considering that. It'll give your mum and me a bit of space and independence.'

Nick clicked on to the next set of photographs to show her the tiny private balcony.

'And it's bound to be family run too. These little places normally are. You know your mum, she'd much prefer to stay somewhere quirky with a local touch rather than some tourist hotel.'

The décor was a bit old-fashioned but the main rooms of the apartment were large and light, and sea-facing. It would be such a treat for her mother to be right on the sea, yet Cally still looked uncertain.

'Yes, I suppose. It just looks a bit functional rather than cosy.'

'It will be fine,' Nick said firmly. 'I think it will give us exactly the space, peace and flexibility we want.'

An added attraction for Nick was the lack of WiFi, a bonus for the getting-away-from-it-all holiday he had in mind. His Chambers would be informed of his absence and Cally could be trusted to keep a watchful eye on Alice's email account. Pomegranates, the party catering Alice helped to cook for, would be starting to fill up her diary for the summer months.

* * *

For most of the Eurostar journey from London Alice was convinced that Paris, the city of romance, must be their destination. But then she remembered that Nick had told her to pack shorts and sun-cream, which did not seem appropriate for chilly April.

During the taxi ride across Paris to Orly Airport she tried to prise more information from him.

'Not telling,' he said but she could see he was pleased to be asked.

Now, sitting opposite him in the airport bar, she attempted to tease their eventual destination out of him. The departures board showed flights to Quimper, Malta, Lorient, Mauritius, Bordeaux, Ajaccio and Marrakech.

'It must be somewhere warmer than England so that probably rules out Quimper and Bordeaux,' she speculated. 'I'm guessing it's more remote than mainland France, or that you can't fly directly to it from London.'

'Very good, Mrs Stenning! You should've been a detective. You can, in fact, fly straight to our unknown destination, just not this early in the year.'

A typical lawyer's remark, observed Alice, with amusement.

He smiled at her, while looking at her over the top of his reading glasses. Alice could tell he was enjoying the last few minutes that the secret was his alone. She looked at his grizzled but still handsome head with affection as he returned to scanning his newspaper.

She considered the remaining flight options. Mauritius would be heavenly but an unlikely choice for just for one week. Please let it be Marrakech, she wished hard. She had always wanted to go there.

When it was time, Nick shepherded her to the gate displaying the Air France flight to Ajaccio. She registered a shockwave of disappointment before adjusting to actuality. So, not Marrakech then.

Ajaccio? Where was that? Italy? She should know. If only her mind wasn't butterflying around so, she'd be able to remember. About to give in and ask Nick in the queue to process boarding passes, she spotted a tourist guide clutched by the hipster-type ahead of them. There was the answer, printed in bold white on the cover. Of course, she recollected, Ajaccio was the capital of Corsica.

Corsica might not be as exotic as Marrakech, nevertheless it was still likely to be an interesting island, she sensibly told herself. She had gone along with the surprise element of the holiday but was beginning to have doubts about doing so. Perhaps abdicating all responsibility to Nick had not been such a good call.

She put on a bright face and said, 'Corsica! How lovely, darling!'

* * *

On top of the early morning Eurostar journey and the taxi dash across Paris, he warned her they faced a long drive up the west coast of the island. Why, she wondered, had he chosen somewhere so far from the airport?

As though Nick read her thoughts, he said: 'You're going to love our mystery hideaway when we get there. I know it! I promise you it'll be worth the journey to be in such a remote spot.'

A broad road stretched away from the airport into the hills, and they sped through pastoral undulations dotted with eucalyptus trees where Alice spotted the first of many lone giant fennels, their tall feathery fronds topped by yellow flower heads. As they went on, she noticed more and more of these enormous fennel plants scattered about, like some sort of horticultural epidemic in the making.

She pointed them out to Nick.

'So many! I think they're waiting to collect themselves and advance triffid-like across the landscape.'

'You do have the most vivid imagination!' he replied with a laugh.

Back down towards the coast, the road described rocky bays of limestone and sand, bright in the early May sunlight, shelving into the foam-fringed turquoise and blue beyond. Inland, to her right, snow crowned the remote mountain-tops which were touched by patchy froths of cloud.

They passed an embryonic ribbon development that would doubtless multiply along the sea road in future years. A small parade of shops, a two star hotel, uniform low-rise flats with balconies then nothing for a few kilometres until they reached a similar coastal strip.

The climb up and away from the sea heralded the start of a narrower road cut into the rock. Low parapets of stonework ran along the outer edge punctuated by gaps, shallow passing bays and occasional viewing points. Limestone gave way to spectacular pink granite cliffs that rose out of land and sea, and glowed a vibrant earthy red where the late afternoon sun warmed their facets.

The harsh edge of the seat belt grazed Alice's neck. She gripped the hand-hold of the car door every time the drops became too dizzying, or when she considered Nick was taking the bends too fast. At any rate he was taking them faster than she would have done. At least, Alice figured, he was nearer the middle of the road than she was on the blind corners, giving him a better view of any oncoming traffic. This is like being locked in the seat of a fairground ride, Alice thought as she felt herself thrown first to one side of the car, then the other, with no end in sight.

The Corsicans seemed to delight in driving at them with their car wheels hanging over the white markings, invading the Citroen's space, then pulling back over the line with inches to spare as if surprised to find another car on the road. Motorbike cavalcades that grouped menacingly in her wing mirror, waiting to swerve and roar past them, were no less frightening. Nor were the streams of Lycra-clad cyclists riding the island's relentless bends. They all unnerved her.

Alice could sense Nick's mild irritation but could not conquer her apprehension fully.

'Look at the flowers and the scenery instead', he told her.

The landscape was indeed lovely. The hills were covered in dense low shrubs bright tipped with season's new growth. *Maquis*, Nick told her, was the local name for this type of flora. He must have been reading up on the island in preparation, she realised. How he loved guidebooks and maps! She was sure there would be a stash of them hidden in his luggage.

The herbs, a range of greys, greens, whites and yellows, and the flowering shrubs were glorious in the spring sunshine but she was frequently pulled back from her enjoyment of the beauty around her by Nick's sudden braking, or her perceived need to be an extra pair of eyes on a hairpin turn.

They stopped briefly in Calvi to stretch their legs and shop for food. The road from there to St. Florent was more forgiving, allowing Alice to free her mind from the road until the last winding stretch up Cap Corse.

It had taken the remainder of the afternoon and all evening to wiggle northwards from Ajaccio. Why do I feel so weary? Alice wondered, especially since Nick was doing all the driving. Maybe this was another symptom of middle-age, or just exhaustion caused by tense hours trapped in the car on horribly scary roads. Nick had insisted they do all the travelling in one day so he could relax fully during the coming week. She did see the point, after all it was his holiday too.

She tallied the days of holiday ahead of them. Today was Thursday, so they had Friday, Saturday, Sunday, Monday, Tuesday and Wednesday ahead of them before travelling back the following Thursday. Six whole days, and Nick had promised that there was a quicker, straighter route they could take on the way back.

'I wanted to bring you on the coastal route because I'd read that the west side of the island is outstanding. I wanted your first experience of Corsica to be special,' he told her. She squeezed his knee to show that she appreciated his thoughtfulness, at least.

Just before midnight she finally spotted the sign Nick had asked her to look out for. The sign that read Marina du Roc Noir. Nick swung the car off the road and down a track leading to the sea's edge, past a hunch of houses, washed ghostly white in the headlights, round the corner to the beach, where the road ran out. To their left, set into the cliff face slightly above them, stood the Relais de la Mer, a lone two storey building mounted on a rocky platform hanging over the sea.

Nick ran the Citroen up the short slope of driveway, steered the car into the single parking bay and cut the engine. Even before they could undo their seatbelts and climb out of the car the roaring crash of wave against stone and rock invaded the vehicle, replacing the noise of the motor with the sound of an immensely more powerful force.

Tired and hungry as she was, Alice thought the Relais looked surreal and unwelcoming in the moonlight. Once out of the vehicle, gusts of wind carried the salt tang to her nostrils, and she studied what she could see of the bay from the parapet of the driveway. In the eerie light, the dark thrashing waves were tipped with luminous foam where the waters thrust towards her. She sensed the bay had a desolate kind of beauty.

She meant it genuinely when she turned towards Nick and said, 'I can see why you chose this place.'

'Wait until tomorrow when you can see it in the daylight. It's very beautiful in a rugged, striking sort of way.'

'I'm sure.'

'Oh, and I think you'll be pleased to know that

we have a whole apartment to ourselves here. Don't expect great luxury but it looks comfortable enough. I decided being right on the sea was too special to miss. It does look a little bleak tonight but I'm sure it will suit us fine.'

She looked up at the unlit exterior of the Relais and decided there was nothing cheerful about this featureless bunker of a building hunkered into the cliff-face. Dark and shuttered, it looked grey and bleak in the moonlight.

'Come on, let's get inside,' Nick prompted her gently.

Alice focused her attention on unloading the food and luggage.

The outside steps to the first floor were starkly outlined by moonlight at the bottom, and as she went up the way ahead was indicated by the electric glow leaking through the reeded glass entrance door. A lamp had been left on for them inside and, as Nick had arranged with the owner, the door was unlocked. Once through the door, Nick turned on the main light in the corridor.

'Keep going until you reach the end,' said Nick.

Alice led the way, wheeling her hand-luggage. They passed a row of identical empty bedrooms overlooking the sea, with numbered doors ajar and a cork tag dangling from the key in each lock. Opposite these were doors to a bathroom and toilet, and further down the passageway, a choice of two unmarked doors, one on the bathroom side, one straight ahead. Feeling shattered and without thinking properly, Alice tried the first door she came to, the one on her left, and ended up on a tiny back balcony facing the cliff that housed, as far as she could tell in the dimness, a clothes drier, a bucket and a mop.

She felt foolish and flustered for making such a silly mistake. Nick would not have done that, she knew. It would have been obvious to him that the door to their accommodation would not be facing the cliff.

'Silly me!'

She opened the remaining door, found the light switch, flipped it on and abandoned her bag to explore their quarters.

The apartment was charmless but large, clean and functional. A long hallway connected a kitchen, bedroom and living room, all of generous dimensions. The living room, which doubled as a dining area, had a prominent brick fireplace and a big picture window looking out to sea. French doors faced sideways along the bay. Alice put her face to the door glass, moulding her hands round her eyes to shut out the light from the room, and saw that the doors opened on to a narrow strip of a balcony.

Nick turned on the electric wall heaters in the bedroom and living room to take the chill off those rooms.

'Just going to slip the latch on the outer door now we have some keys,' he called down the hallway as he removed the keys and cork tag from the lock. He returned to help Alice unpack their supermarket purchases: eating was their next priority. Sitting down to a late supper chased down with numbing French brandy cheered Alice considerably. It quickly made the place feel less other, more like their own.

That's a start, she reasoned, but it's just as well I packed my hot water bottle. She was glad she'd brought a bit of cosy homeliness with her. Maybe once they had settled in, populated the place with their belongings, and seen it in daylight, it would appear less depressing. Less like a mistake.

II The Stay

It was wonderful to wake to the sound of the sea below their window, Alice contemplated sleepily from under the extra blankets on her side of the bed. The repeated sucking back of water before the drawn out roll of the next wave was one of her favourite things, a sound that never failed to lift her heart and make her glad to be alive.

She eased herself out of bed, careful not to disturb Nick who needed to sleep off yesterday's long drive, and slipped her feet into her flip-flops to avoid contact with the cold tiled floor. Her cardigan had had to serve as a bed jacket over her strappy shift. She remembered wistfully how she'd packed the slip of silk and lace, sexy and subtle as the inside of an oyster shell. Perhaps she had been over-optimistic in expecting a more lavish bedroom, a room where the temperature could be racked up in more ways than one.

Looking over to Nick's recumbent figure, his expression sweet and boyish in sleep, she smiled to herself and left him be. There would be plenty other occasions to spend time together over the coming days. She looked forward to re-forging the greater depth of connection, the heightened passion only reached by her when pressures and demands were left miles and a world behind.

Alice pulled her navy fleece on top of the cardigan, killing any thought of desire with it.

She paused a second or two by the mirror and assessed what it had to tell her. The straight blonde hair still carried something of the flicked-out style coaxed into it by her hairdresser, who expertly covered Alice's greys every few weeks, adjusting mousiness into a colour more flattering to her fading skin tone. A few flicks with her hairbrush corrected the stray sticking out bits. She moved closer to the mirror, licked her forefinger to erase the sooty smear of eyeliner and mascara that had crept down to unacceptable levels below her green-grey eyes, the residue of last night's hasty make-up removal, until a more flattering echo of yesterday's outlines remained.

'Another year older,' she murmured.

Still, her figure was slim, well-proportioned and passable in clothes. She had never been a beauty. Her girlfriends labelled her facial features attractive rather than pretty, although she possessed physical attributes that many wished they had. Being consistently happy with her looks eluded Alice but today was a good day, she could see her younger self in her reflection. Plenty of water on the journey and a good sleep had kept her skin hydrated. She shrugged at the Alice in the mirror and moved on.

In the sitting room she drifted to the picture window, pulled up the handle and opened it out on its hinges, the better to see the view and let in the sea's clamour.

Alice loved the view immediately.

Layers of cloud hung over the little bay but farther out to sea the sky was a clear, tantalising azure. Dark rocks showed through the blue-grey water below the window where waves rolled, glowing the turquoise-bright of glacier ice, and broke on the jagged shore releasing the seawater into bubbling white foam.

Then she saw it, rising up at the far end of the bay. She hadn't noticed it when they arrived last night, hadn't known to look. Nick had only told her about it over supper last night, and in any case, she figured, in the darkness its stone profile would probably have been absorbed into the rock face behind. But now there it was. The tower.

She remembered he'd said that it was one of the many Genoese round towers constructed in the 16th and 17th centuries to defend the Corsican coast from Barbary pirates.

Her heart lightened. Clever Nick! She conceded his choice of this place was inspired.

* * *

Nick found her, an hour later, her hands cupped round an empty tea mug, happily absorbed by the view.

'Hello, love.'

He bent to kiss the top of her head and was rewarded by her upturned smiling face as she stretched her arms to gather him to her for a proper kiss, the mug still in one hand.

He knew she loved the sea with the passionate, dependant love born out of a childhood lived in a Sussex Cinque port. She had often tried to explain the pull of such a big, wild body of water; the coastal palate of blues, greens, mauves, greys, tans and honey tones, black, and shades of white; the sharp scent of salt and seaweed on the wind; the harsh, urgent cry of gulls arcing across the water. Although Nick was more at home in the English countryside, during the thirty years they had been married he had caught some of Alice's enthusiasm for seascapes and enjoyed them not just for their natural beauty but also for the positive effect they had on her. Their arrival at any seaside destination transformed her default expression of seriousness into something warmer and more alive. Joy turned her back into a younger version of herself, more fun-loving and easy-going than she had been in recent years.

'Are you all right staying here? We could always find somewhere else,' he said.

Alice understood the reassurance he was seeking from her, the need to hear her confirm he'd chosen well.

'No, it's fine and it has everything we need. The setting is lovely and so peaceful, if you don't count the sea! It's a treat to be right by the water and to hear that roar.'

Nick probably expected that answer but she noticed he still looked relieved.

'How about breakfast, a look around here and then a walk into the village?' he suggested. 'It's only about four kilometres away.'

'Great! I'll go and have a quick shower and get dressed.'

Alice rose from her seat by the window and paused, looking directly at him.

'Actually, I've got a better plan.'

She shrugged off the fleece and cardigan in one easy movement, letting them fall to the floor. One strap of the silken slip slid down her arm. She couldn't have done it better.

'Let's christen the bed properly before we do anything else.'

* * *

The contrast between their arrival and this morning was marked. Today, in the daylight and seduced by the view, everything seemed beautiful and full of promise – just as the start of a holiday should feel.

Flushed and happy from their love-making, Alice drained her coffee mug, cleared their plates away and set off with Nick to explore the rest of the Relais and its surroundings.

The exterior of the building was coated in a granular, grey effect, some sort of specialist masonry finish beyond Alice's knowledge or interest. In the bright morning light the window frames and shutters radiated a lurid aquamarine glow, not visible in last night's darkness.

'I'm certain that the core of this building is an old boathouse with the bed and breakfast rooms and private quarters below built on at a later date,' said Nick, pointing at the slippery cobbled ramp from the terrace to the sea.

'Do you know, I think you're right!' Alice was impressed. She'd never have spotted it herself, but once he said it, it seemed obvious.

On the ground floor of the extension she tried but failed to open the glass-panelled door decorated with colourful stickers advertising water sports and nearby restaurants. Behind it she could make out an office area, a low brown couch, and a wall-mounted TV clearly for use by the owner and his family.

'I suppose if we are the only guests and we don't need breakfast made for us, there's no need for anyone to be around all the time,' she said looking at the deserted tables and chairs on the covered terrace. She tried to imagine the place in high season sprinkled with couples in their summer clothes, or busy in the evening with additional tourists dropping by for a glass or two of *cap corse* or *muscat* from the tiny outdoor bar and perhaps staying for a barbeque supper.

A light wind sped the bulk of the clouds inland. Sunlight filtered down, casting faint shadows where the remaining vapours thinned and parted.

Her eye was caught by a rangy black cat running low and fast across the terrace. It paused, looking back over its shoulder past the rusty grill racks set in brick and the string of grubby fairy lights, as if assessing some perceived threat. Then, satisfied, it moved on at a slower pace to crouch in the shadow of a hopeful young palm tree, potted in terracotta; one of several, alternating with young tamarisks, behind which a white rail and post fence edged the drop to the black beach below.

Such a mixture this place between clean neatness and almost desolation, mused Alice, as she moved forward to commune with the cat.

She squatted to greet it. Close to, the animal did not meet her aesthetic expectations. It had a slightly tattered appearance, not helped by the breeze ruffling its fur, but its most notable feature was a pair of intense orange eyes that stared up at her disconcertingly. Alice froze a moment, then remembered to blink at the cat as a sign of friendly greeting. But the cat remained unmoved, declining to return her gesture. Surprised to be unnerved by the hostility of its gaze, Alice straightened and retreated from its forbidding glare.

She caught up with Nick on the driveway and they rounded the corner together towards a group of little houses tucked back on the roadside.

The black rock beach between the Relais and the tower was split by a small river, wide enough to require a narrow stone bridge near its mouth, and to need a wider bridge further upstream to carry the coastal road on and up the Cap.

'We can go over this footbridge towards the tower, which is where the footpath to the road starts,' Nick showed the way with his finger. 'It cuts out the loop of road behind the bay.'

'Can I go down to the water's edge, first? It's so near.'

Alice mentally ticked herself off as she said the words. Why sound so unassertive? She didn't need his permission. I must work on being more affirmative in future, she told herself.

'It doesn't look very easy to me,' Nick responded. 'Have a go if you like. I'll sit here and wait.'

He climbed over the stone parapet to sit on a crop of smooth black rocks on the seaward side. The distance to the sea was short but Alice had to pick her way down through slopes and troughs of elliptic grey-black stones. The going was painstakingly slow. Arms outstretched to help her balance, she wobbled and hesitated before each step. The sea might as well be miles away for all the progress she was making. Tears of frustration threatened to obscure her sight.

Nick intervened. 'Come back, Alice before you twist an ankle,' he yelled after her.

She wiped her eyes with the back of her hand and turned back awkwardly. Nick came forward to meet her, offering a steady hand.

'Well, we've established that this is not the right kind of beach for a casual stroll,' he said, attempting humour to lighten her disappointment. 'But there are plenty of sandy coves for us to explore nearby. Come, let's go get going towards the village.'

Approaching the footbridge, they drew nearer to the houses grouped by the roadside. The assortment of fifteen or so buildings ranged from old stone dwellings with wooden shutters and overlapping roof slates, to modern boxes with iron railed balconies, metal shutters and factory-made roof tiles — more practical, but with little in the way of character about them. What all the properties had in common was evidence of occupation accompanied by a sense of inwardness. An elderly car was parked outside one house, an empty pushchair by the door of another, a pair of rush-bottomed chairs waited for occupants on a bare patio above them, a washing line festooned with pastel coloured plastic pegs ready to do their duty. Yet all was silent; doors closed and shutters drawn.

Halfway across the footbridge, Alice turned to look back and met the eyes of a thickset woman with a short shock of hair standing on one of the roof terraces. Probably she was a similar age to Alice but life and circumstances made her seem older. Alice gave her a smile but the woman looked away and turned to go back inside her house.

When she remarked on it, Nick said lightly, 'I expect you've made her day. She has probably gone to tell her husband that she's spotted the first tourist of the summer.'

She let a small noise escape her throat to signify assent, although in her heart she could not go along with his jokey explanation. She believed the woman was watching them resentfully and that her intent was no friendlier than the cat's.

At the far side of the bridge, the stonework of the tower, restored in parts, flared upwards into a portly waist pinched in by a stone course. Arrow slits faced only towards the beach side.

'You need to imagine a lookout in the battlements above us blowing a large conch,' said Nick who'd been busy studying local history over his breakfast. 'The sound would've been like the prolonged moan of a foghorn, warning the local populace to flee inland from approaching raiders.'

He showed Alice the tower's door placed at first floor level at the back, its only access by ladder, of which there was none to be seen.

She tried to conjure up a mental image of the imminent danger to which Nick alluded but in the warm sunlight the tower looked benign. Whatever events it had witnessed remained locked in the past.

Blood-bright poppies blew above the sparse, sun-bleached grasses that sprouted along the stony edge of the steep footpath to the coast road. Not good at heights, Alice was pushed almost to the limits of her bravery by the right-hand drop to the thin ribbon of water below. Her heart pulsed a beat of doom in her ear, threatening her complete concentration on the narrow strip of beaten earth in front of her feet. Getting to the top without being overcome with panic was all she could focus on. She was very relieved when they reached the broad asphalt platform of the road.

At first all was quiet as Nick led the way, keeping to the outer edge of the road to face any approaching traffic. Alice found it unnerving to walk the stretches with only ankle-high walls, or no barrier at all, between her and the steep plunge.

'Keep to the edge,' commanded Nick, aware of Alice walking close to the centre of the road. 'Anything coming towards us is going to be moving fast.'

But she was more scared of the drop and how

easy it would be to make a mistake, to trip over her own feet. She trusted the driver of any vehicle to brake in time more than she trusted herself to win her own battle with disequilibrium and poor co-ordination.

The first few road bends allowed a view of the way ahead and they were passed with consideration by the two cars they encountered, but the gentle curves turned into tortuous, blind corners.

'Bit disappointing,' said Nick. 'We'll have to turn back. Never mind, we'll go and get the car and drive there.'

'OK, but I am not going back down that track. Going up's one thing but I can't do it coming down.'

'But it's much further.'

'I don't care. You go the short way, I'll meet you back there.'

Nick did not argue and peeled off down the beach path. Alice picked up her pace, keen to prove that while her route might be longer, the detour did not take much extra time. Besides, they were on holiday. What was the rush?

Immediately after the road bridge, barking - sudden and loud, spooked her momentarily until the source of the rowdiness became visible - three cocky-looking tan and white mongrels in assorted sizes chained to a lone house wedged between the riverbank and the road. Confined to the property's frontage by their bonds, they did their worst. They jumped right up on to the roadside wall and issued noisy proprietorial statements that, amplified by the hills, quelled the birdsong.

When Alice was tiny, an over-boisterous German Shepherd had left her terrified of dogs for years, yet she had gradually trained herself to be rational on the occasions she encountered them. Time had taught her the chances of any hostility or aggression were, on the whole, unlikely, so she understood these dogs for what they were but, nevertheless, was glad to be on the far side of the road. She carried on the last short stretch before it met the track and descended to the Relais, where she might possibly spot Nick below her.

But before she reached the track the small fright the dogs had given her was nothing compared to the heart-lurch she felt in her chest now and the hot prickling of rising panic.

She had not seen them initially, their cages hidden by the confusing sun-and-shade patterns thrown by the nearest trees, until a guttural growling quickly backed up by deep aggressive barking, full of intent, triggered her fear. She had a quick impression of powerful brindled bodies, pugnacious heads, merciless eyes and ferocious teeth as the beasts chucked themselves toward the wire, towards her. A gnome-like figure, hovering by the structure that housed the pens, turned to see who had disturbed his charges. He laughed when he saw her, seeming to enjoy her visible terror; his broken teeth were as shiny with saliva as those of the dogs, his eyes bright and glittery, fixed on hers.

Alice ran and did not stop until she was halfway down to the sea.

* * *

On her way back Alice rehearsed telling Nick what had happened and imagined being comforted by exclamations of 'How awful!' and 'Poor love!' But she knew that in reality this type of sympathy would be elicited only from her girlfriends. Nick would more likely say, 'Interesting. Must be hunting dogs. I wonder what breed?'

These fancies were driven from her head by the sight of Nick on the Relais terrace absorbed in conversation with a dark–haired man. The stranger's slender back was turned towards her.

'Y at-il beaucoup de tempêtes en hiver?'

Without any attempt at an accent, Nick addressed his question to the other man, who looked to be in his early thirties, about half Nick's age. Alice, joining them, assessed the relaxed manner of the stranger — white shirt sleeves rolled up to display brown forearms, hands in the pockets of his tight black jeans. It must be the owner of the Relais, she decided. Nick had mentioned him earlier. Bruno Franticelli. He might have been handsome but for his craggy nose and the left eye that had turned milky, like that of a long–dead fish.

Alice felt out of kilter, forced to forego recounting the story of her recent dramas and stand patiently at Nick's side. The Corsican nodded to her in acknowledgement and gave Nick a leisurely reply accompanied by shoulder shrugs. Her French had never been good but she understood the gist of it – 'Yes, the winter storms were frequent, bad and often did plenty of damage.'

Bruno turned his one dark eye on her, his manner polite but uninterested in her as a woman.

'Tout va bien? Avez-vous tout ce dont vous avez besoin?' he asked.

'Oui, l'appartement est très bien. Merci.'

'C'est parfait, et bien je vous laisse. Au revoir.' He extracted one hand from its imprisonment and waved it aloft in farewell as he turned quickly and went into the office.

'Bit odd,' said Nick as they headed towards the car. 'He says he's off somewhere for the next few days so I've paid him in cash and he's told us to leave the key in the door when we go, if he's not back. Apparently, we are the only ones staying here this week.'

'I'm quite glad he's not around. He's a little on the creepy side.'

'He can't help how he looks,' said Nick. 'Actually, I thought he was perfectly fine.'

His matter of fact acceptance made her wish she had kept her thoughts to herself. He made her feel ashamed that she had appeared judgemental.

'I wonder if there is a Madame Franticelli tucked away somewhere?' she said to shift the subject to safer ground.

* * *

The village was of no great size, strung out along the coast road, with its centre clinging to a pinnacle of rock which created a pinch-point for the traffic. Cars, motorbikes and mega coaches backed up on either side of the narrow gap, waiting their turn to pass. Further chaos ensued from a vehicle that was shadowing one of the few parking spaces, waiting for it to be liberated.

'It's so busy here! Why?'

Alice flattened her back against the wall of a house to avoid being clipped by a wing mirror.

'Well, remember this is the only road in the village as well the scenic route round the Cap, plus it has its own attractions.' Nick waved his arm in the direction of a church ahead of them. 'This place, for example, has quite a story attached to it.'

Nick propelled her out of the way of the traffic and on to the steps of the church of Sainte Julie.

'Let's take a look and I'll tell you what I've read.'

The church's vibrant façade was set back from the road and reached by a long flight of steps.

'What an extraordinary colour!' Alice looked up at the edifice, classical in style with a square tower, and tried to think if she'd ever see a church painted pinky-orange before.

Nick held the door open for her and she plunged into the chilly dark of the interior. Despite the busyness outside, the church's only other occupants were a trio of head-scarfed grannies dotted about the front row of chairs. The Stennings moved down the aisle towards the baroque altar, Nick all the while recounting in a loud whisper the story of Sainte Julie.

'Julie was a Carthaginian Christian girl on her

way to Gaul to be sold as a slave in the fifth century. The slavers docked their ship here while a pagan festival was in progress - you know, sacrificing bulls on the beach and whatnot. Julie refused to participate and so she was tortured and crucified. Then it's hard to separate fact from legend – and this is rather gruesome, but apparently her breasts were cut off and thrown on to a stone.'

Alice shivered in sympathy for the girl's horrible fate but not being religious herself she found herself torn between admiring the young girl's stance and not fully comprehending the need to die for one's faith. Despite a glare from one of the women in the seats at the front, Nick carried on.

'From that stone, two springs of water flowed. They are now enshrined in the chapel down on the beach and Julie has become the patron saint of Corsica.'

'I think I need some lunch after that tale! Can we go and find somewhere with tables outside?'

Alice was keen to head out in the warm sunshine again and leave the old women in peace.

Nick suggested she might like to choose between the tiny terraced bistrot and an open-air café bar built on layers of crazy-patterned stone round a waterless fountain, its tables and chairs shaded by plane and fig trees.

Alice plumped for the sunnier Bistrot d'Antoine. A stocky little man greeted them on the threshold, introducing himself as the proprietor, Antoine. He shook the Stennings' hands forcefully before steering them to the best corner table on the little raised terrace. This provided a comfortable vantage point from which they could observe the street chaos with a measure of enjoyment derived from their elevated detachment behind railings and planters of fluorescent pink geraniums.

'Look at that dog. He knows his way around.' Alice pointed out a splodged and spotted hound that wove its way through the traffic and drifts of tourists, deftly avoiding the oncoming scooters and bikes attempting a similar dance through the larger obstructions.

Antoine, who it seemed was also the waiter for whole establishment, swiftly produced large glasses of wine, a carafe of water and a basket of bread to keep them going while they studied the menu.

His English was fairly good. He stopped to chat, encouraged by Nick asking if he'd ever been to England. He told them that he had worked in London hotels in the Eighties and had been back a couple of times since. Once he and Nick had established common reference points - favourite restaurants in the capital - Antoine wanted to know where they were staying. He frowned when they told him, the heavy lines across his forehead folding to new depths.

'Franticelli! He shut the Relais, maybe five years ago after Vanina, his wife, ran off. Gone, disappeared but perhaps he comes back now,' he said, raking the fingers of one hand through his grey-threaded hair as if agitated by the news. '*Je ne sais pas*. Me, I close at the end of the season. Go back to Ajaccio. Travel. Last year, Relais still closed. How you say? Dead-end? Yes, dead-end down there. No-one, I mean no-one, goes there.'

'Well, nevertheless that is where we're staying,' said Nick. 'We met Bruno this morning. He even has a website for the place. That's how we found it. We are the only ones there but that's not surprising if he's only just got started again.'

Antoine raised an eyebrow. 'My sister, Martina, she lived at the Relais one summer, cleaning, doing beds but now she's in St. Florent so this is news to me.'

He took their order and bustled off.

'So Bruno's wifeless! Unless he's found another woman, or what's-her-name's come back?'

'Vanina.' Nick frowned a little.

Alice could feel his disapproval of her curiosity beaming across the table at her. It was the sort of conversation she could have with a girlfriend at home but not with Nick. He hated gossip. She mentally kicked herself for saying anything. She decided to let it go for the moment but if there was another chance to coax more out of Antoine later, she would take it. In the meantime she knew a charm offensive was required if the mood was going to be sweet over lunch.

Alice raised her glass inviting Nick to join her in a toast. 'Here's to a great holiday. Thank you, darling, for organising it.'

They clinked their glasses of rosé together in a upward motion as if by doing so they could will the next few days to be perfect.

'After lunch we could take a look at the remains

of the fortress here before going down to the chapel on the beach. It'll be a bit of climb up afterwards. Six hundred steps but it will be worth it. It's a rather unusual beach.'

Nick opened his guidebook at the place he'd marked with a sticker at breakfast time, and showed Alice a colour photograph - a panoramic view of a bay taken from a great height. The sea, the vivid royal blue of ink, gave way to bright turquoise before reaching the surprisingly black sand.

Alice had no curiosity about why the sand was that colour. She would have accepted it as fact but she knew Nick was about to tell her.

'The sand's been stained black by asbestos waste from a mine further up the coast. The mine's disused now.'

'Isn't that rather dangerous?' Alice imagined that just by walking along the beach she would kick up tiny particles of asbestos dust and inhale them.

'Apparently not. The locals take their children down there.'

A lunch of sautéed scallops and large glasses of wine did much to restore the holiday spirit, rather battered by the aborted walk, Alice's canine encounters and Nick's stuffiness about the Bruno story. They lingered over their expressos, spinning out a shared glass of aquavit flavoured with myrtle berries.

The wandering dog, friendly but unwelcome, ventured up the short flight of steps towards Nick and Alice's table and was shooed away forcefully

by Antoine, playing out a drama that Alice
suspected was repeated several times a day.

When he presented their bill Antoine paused to
chat to them again, free from the necessity of
serving anyone else at the now empty tables.

Nick and he were back on the favourite
restaurant theme, which migrated to favourite
dishes before Alice, mellow from the lunch, sought
to join in and redirect the conversation.

'I saw some penned dogs this morning above
our beach. They were large and very fierce.' She
waved towards Nick. 'My husband says they must
be kept for hunting. Is that right?'

'Dark-hair? Some with white on their fronts and
feets?' asked Antoine, his English a little stretched
now.

Alice nodded.

'Ah! *Cursinu*, sounds like. For guarding,
gathering cattle, and yes, hunting *sanglier*. Good to
their owners but not so friendly with *les étrangers*.
Like many countries there is sometimes trouble
here with dog fights for sport and money.'

She shuddered at such cruelty, imagining a
crowd of bestial men, the owners egging on their
dogs to attack each other until one fatally injured,
or destroyed the other. She chased away the
unwelcome images in her head with the last
mouthful of aquavit.

'Oh. You see Franticelli's eye?' added Antoine as
an afterthought, pointing to one of his own. 'She
did that. Vanina. She had her reasons but both of
them were trouble.'

'Really?' asked Alice, now fascinated and

hoping for more detail. She leant forward, rested her head on her elbow and twisted her body round towards Antoine to block out any chance of catching Nick's eye. She looked up the man, willing him to say more.

Antoine paused for a moment. Alice wondered if he was dismissing her as a nosy tourist and would clam up but, no, it seemed he was merely summoning the right words in his rusty English.

'Vanina was from Bastia. She and Bruno married quick. The father of Bruno, César Franticelli, he's nasty little man but strong. Lives in one of those houses by the Relais with his wife, Saveria. Used to beat Bruno when he was an *enfant* like one of his dogs, *peut-être* it's César's dogs you talk about. Maybe he beats Saveria too. Her father, her mother they die when Saveria was young girl. They leave her a house for the boats and a little money. Big, big mistake to marry César. He use her money to make the Relais. She had no more family and then there was little Bruno, so she stay with César.'

'I knew it was a boathouse!' Nick said with satisfaction, Alice noted, despite his dislike for tittle-tattle.

'So, what happened to Bruno and Vanina?' Alice was keen to hear more.

'César and Saveria move to little house nearby and let Bruno and Vanina run the Relais. César not like Vanina much. She was, how do you say, strong in the mind.'

'Strong-minded? Independent?' offered Alice.

'Yes, yes,' replied Antoine a little impatiently.

'Like I said. There is more. She had big ideas. Thought she was too smart to help at the Relais. César made trouble between them, so Bruno, he get unhappy with Vanina, start drinking too much, spending money on motorbikes, women. One day she says she hates César, hates the Relais – it gives her bad dreams. Bruno, he laughs. Hits her around. My sister, Martina, she sees it all. Vanina, she takes a pen and puts it Bruno's eye.'

Antoine removed a ballpoint pen from behind one ear and mimed stabbing motions, with such gusto that Nick shrank back into his chair.

'Bruno, he holds his face like this,' Antoine cradled one eye and cheek with in his hands and bent over groaning. 'Vanina, she runs with my sister. They don't go back.'

'Goodness, what a story.' It certainly added colour to their stay at the Relais but Alice was relieved that Bruno would be away for the rest of the week.

* * *

'Hi, Mum. How is it?'

The disembodied voice of Cally from the smartphone pressed to her ear sounded young and cheerful. Alice pictured Cally sitting at the kitchen table in her Saturday running kit, the long straight pale hair pulled back from her elfin face and fastened into a high ponytail with a twist of elastic.

'It's lovely, darling. Your Dad and I are sitting in the sunshine by the harbour in St. Florent and we've just polished off two huge bowlfuls of pasta with wild boar *ragout*.'

'Lucky you! It sounds heavenly.'

'Sorry, we haven't called you before but the apartment we're staying in is a bit out of the way. There's no signal there.'

'How do you like the place?'

'Our apartment's a bit basic but it's in a lovely setting right by the sea. Dad said he showed you the website, remember?'

'Oh, yes… Mum, remind me, which day are you back?'

'Thursday, darling, so we'll see you late evening if you are around.' Alice kept it casual. Six months into her first job, Cally's starting salary at the ad agency necessitated her living at home, but Alice knew better than to make her feel pinned down. They had all had to adjust when she returned from her studies at Newcastle, three years older and used to independent living. Alice waved at Nick to get his attention, and asked,

'Do you want to say hello to Dad?'

* * *

They walked inland that afternoon, leaving the car in a lay-by at the Roc Noir road bridge to navigate a pathway hugging the hillside, spotted by Nick on the map. It led eventually to a ridge before dropping down to a village on the other side. They never intended to go the whole way but just to enjoy an off-road amble before going back to relax.

Aware of Alice's problem with heights, Nick assured her they could give up at any point if she was uncomfortable.

'Actually, it looks fine. It's not narrow and it looks like there are trees and bushes all the way up. It's sheer drops I don't like,' she said, wondering, as she often did, if Nick was listening properly.

As she predicted, the going was fine and the incline gentle. They walked for nearly an hour through a corridor of abundant vegetation with occasional breaks of bare rock as they climbed higher, pausing at one of these sunlit patches to watch a lone bird of prey, its wing feathers stretched into bent fingers, dip and glide above the trees of the opposite hillside.

At the top of the ridge, parallel with the distant sea, they stopped to admire the view over the mass of tree cover that rolled below them like puffy clouds of blue-green broccoli. The path then took them slightly downwards to a heavily wooded section where the sun did not penetrate. They walked on through an abandoned settlement of roofless, partially-overgrown stone dwellings jammed up against the rock face.

'It seems an odd place to live, on a slope like this,' said Alice.

'Remember none of these trees would have been here then, they've grown up in and around the ruins,' said Nick. 'Somewhere around them will be the remains of cultivable terraces originally planted with vines probably.'

Alice thought of the conch-blower warning of the approaching raiders. Would the men, women and children of the coast flee up this path to here, or to villages beyond? Surely, the invaders could easily follow? Maybe they had hiding places in the surrounding hillsides? What would it be like to be crouched undercover and fearful as the pirates carried off what they could find, including hundreds of Corsicans to sell or use as slaves? When would it be safe to come out? Who, or what would be missing and how long until the next raid?

She asked Nick what else he could remember from his prolonged reading sessions about the history of the island.

'Sometime towards the end of the fifteenth century the piracy became so bad that people stopped living on the coast and moved inland to villages,' he said. 'The Genoese build the watchtowers, nearly a hundred in all, with paid watchmen to warn the villagers. It seems they evolved a beacon system, lighting fires that could alert the whole island within an hour.'

'More efficient than conch-shells, I suppose,' said Alice.

The heat felt oppressive. The exertion of walking, mostly uphill on a warm afternoon and the lack of breeze under the trees began to tell on Alice. The foliage closed in on her, edging her towards claustrophobia. Even the birds were silent.

They reached the last of the forlorn houses, its gaping shell below them. Alice stopped to look down, her feet level with where the roof would have pitched upwards. She could see the floor partially layered with debris made indistinguishable by a shroud of moss and small plant growth. There was something primeval about the creep of vegetation over what was once a home. She shuddered.

Her hand flew to cover her nose as a rotten stench reached her nostrils. When she turned her head to follow her nose, the source of the stink was soon apparent. In front of her, the head of a goat was impaled on a stubby tree branch, eyeless. Swags of dried bloodied skin and flesh hung from below the sockets, as if the ghastly matter was melting from the cheekbones. Coarse tufts of dun-brown hair remained in place between the ridged curlicue horns as did a straggly beard, partly matted with blackened blood. Half the animal's long white teeth showed on one side of its face where the flesh had been eaten away.

Transfixed for a moment, Alice took a swift step backwards, nearly falling down into the sunken house as she collided with Nick. Their movement disturbed a cloud of flies busy with their booty, and sent them buzzing haphazardly into the air. Alice felt one brush her cheek and let rip the scream she'd managed to suppress up until now.

She turned and pushed past Nick in her panic to get away from the horror, and fled back along the path.

* * *

'Don't be silly,' said Nick, not unkindly when they were back in the sunlight. 'There's nothing sinister about it at all. I'm sure a local has just stuck it up there for a bit of fun. An embellishment, even.

Remember when it's finished decomposing, all that will be left is a bleached skull with horns, just like you'd find in a curio shop.'

She knew he was likely to be right. She had overreacted out of fright. How likely was it, really, that the goat's head had been set up as a warning to intruders?

'Well, anyway, isn't it time we got back?'

Alice had had enough of these lonely hills sheltering their deserted ruins, leaving so little imprint of past deeds, refusing to reveal the secrets in their keeping. She needed to be back in the open with the reassuring sights and sounds of civilisation in strong evidence.

* * *

Their evenings had fallen into a pattern of eating in the apartment. It suited them for the time being. Staying out most of the day meant they were pleased to go back, make themselves a cup of tea and read their books and magazines to the accompaniment of the sea before opening a bottle of wine. Saturday evening was warm enough to recline in the loungers on the terrace, a glass of white wine for Alice and a bottle of beer for Nick on the low table between them, as they watched the sun slide down towards the sea.

Alice had become so used to them being the only ones at the Relais that she was surprised by the mind-filling sound of a powerful motorbike approaching. She turned in her lounger, as much as the awkward angle of the seat allowed, and saw a black bike swing round at the top of the incline to park facing back downwards. The leather-clad rider, a tall, slenderly built man, dismounted and briefly looked in their direction, nodded without removing his sleek helmet or raising his black visor and disappeared up the stairway to the first floor. Alice found she rather resented the intrusion. She had come to think of the Relais as their private domain. The metallic smell of hot engine and evaporated petrol drifted across the terrace to where she sat.

'Weren't you told no one else was due to stay here this week?'

But Nick was so lost in his detective book that he had not even registered the arrival of the faceless intruder.

'Probably a last minute booking,' he said vaguely, clearly incurious about the comings and goings of strangers, and keen to return to his novel, but his concentration had lapsed and the evening was taking a chilly turn.

'Time to go in for supper, I think,' he said, tucking his reading glasses into the pocket of his linen shirt and getting up from the chair a little stiffly. He stretched his arms skyward and yawned before scooping up his book and beer bottle.

The bike's metal components emitted pings and tings as they cooled and contracted, catching Alice's attention as they went past.

The second door along on the landing was newly shut, which rather spoiled the symmetry of the corridor, Alice thought. She wondered about the occupant. Who was he? How long would he stay? Why had he picked that particular room out of a row of identical ones? Irrationally, she imagined him lying in the middle of the bed, or standing upright like a statue, still clad in his biker leathers and helmet. Because she had not seen his face, she could not attribute normal human activity - undressing, washing, sleeping – to this man.

Later, getting ready for bed, Nick became slightly tetchy when she remarked that biker had not left the bay all evening, speculating that he had an early supper, tired from his journey.

'Don't you think it strange that he has no luggage with him?' she added rubbing night cream into her skin.

'Sweetheart, I don't know and I couldn't care less. I come on holiday to relax and enjoy myself, not to obsess about passing strangers and their totally uninteresting habits.'

She considered this was a bit unfair and put it down to tiredness because at other times he seemed willing to participate in guessing games about people's motives and actions. She decided to challenge him a little.

'But when you read your thrillers or detective stories you always say you like the mundane detail.'

'Well, obviously that's different. The criminals do things for purposes that become evident later in the story, or the detective does some everyday stuff that reveals his nature and quirks - you know - how they might behave in a given situation. It's fiction so I can take it, or leave it. Real life doesn't have easy explanations, neat endings.

'I may, or may not, see your biker friend tomorrow morning but it is unlikely that I will strike up a lasting relationship with him, even assuming that we speak the same language. If we do talk we'll spend time exchanging details that are liable to be only mildly interesting to either of us and then we will never see each other again.'

He got into bed and turned out the reading light on his side. He was shutting down the conversation but somehow she could not just let it go.

'Where's your sense of curiosity?'

'Darling, you've more than enough for both of us and an overactive imagination to match. We've only been here three days and already we had hostile cats, spooky old ladies, savage dogs…'

'That's not fair! They were savage! You didn't see them, or that horrible old man with them.'

'Ok, sorry, I'll give you that one. What else? Ah yes, sinister landlords and portentous goat heads. Next you'll be telling me you think that our fellow guest is a knife-wielding serial killer! Come here, silly!' He patted the space on the mattress next to his naked body.

She paused, momentarily unsure if she liked his mockery, then deciding to let herself crumble, she laughed and climbed in beside him, tugging the nightgown over her head and discarding it carelessly on the floor as she turned to his arms.

* * *

They were spared any encounter with the mystery

biker the next morning. He remained behind his locked door, Alice noted on their way out to the car.

Today they were off to explore the town of Bastia, a long drive over the other side of the Cap. There they pottered through cool alleyways of shaded shuttered houses, reminding Nick and Alice of other meanders through holiday towns of the Mediterranean – a mixture of decay and glory - peeling paint, washing lines of nylon football shirts drying in company with assorted pastel-coloured sheets and feminine garb, potted greenery tied to balconies, caged birds competing to be heard against radio music or chatter, the sound of voices raised in argument and tantalising wafts of home cooked food that promised to be delicious but never to be eaten by the Stennings.

Driven to hope for something equally mouth-watering for their Sunday lunch, they plumped for a restaurant around the old harbour, choosing one that did not serve the ubiquitous adopted pizza but had more typically rustic fish and meat dishes.

Once their order was placed, Alice asked about the free WiFi mentioned in the menu folder and typed in the password the waiter wrote down for her on a scrap from his order pad. She fiddled with her phone for a bit, scanned her inbox for any important emails, looked at her Facebook newsfeed, and opened a Snapchat from Cally of Tabbicat in a cute pose. She snapped Nick with her phone, smiling, the full beer glass raised to his lips and sent it back to Cally with the caption 'Super-relaxed Dad'.

She opened her usual web browser and ran a search.

'That's odd. I've just looked online for the Relais website and nothing comes up.'

'Why are you looking?' Ever logical, Nick questioned her action.

'I just wanted to see the images on it. You know what it's like when you see photos of a place you've got to know. They can never show quite what it's really like. It's similar but it makes sense in a different way. Like doing a jigsaw puzzle. A piece that's been missing for ages often doesn't look quite like you imagine it should do until you slot it in to position and your mind has to catch up with the altered reality.'

'I think I know what you mean. Are you sure you're typing in the name right?'

'Yes, I've been scrolling about for a while and there's nothing coming up in my searches, no website, no images, no references to it. Nothing. It's as though it doesn't exist.'

'Well, maybe the website's down for some reason. An out-of-the-way place like the Relais probably doesn't have any online history, especially if it has been boarded up for years. It might have even been called something else beforehand. Anyway, put your phone away, here's our lunch.'

The waiter placed the tray transporting their food on an empty table behind them and moved their cutlery until he was satisfied there was sufficient space for the crockery.

'Nothing like the first plate of mussels of the

year.' Nick flicked his napkin open as the man placed a steaming pot in front of him, promising to return with a finger-bowl. Alice had ordered a dish of braised lamb shank with lentils, rice and a side salad. The tender meat fell from the bone easily, the flavour full and satisfying from slow cooking with wine, garlic, vegetables and herbs from the *maquis*. As good and as authentic a meal as any she had smelt in preparation during their morning stroll, she decided.

* * *

'Mmm, this is very pleasant.' Nick's last words before he fell asleep on their travel rug, book open in his outstretched hand and his glasses slightly akimbo. They were on the Plage de la Roya, the strip of sandy beach across the river from St. Florent. Nick had seen it on the map and suggested a postprandial flop there, on the way back from Bastia. Alice, however, was restless. In order to find Nick some head shade they were obliged to be on the edge of a group of pink flowering tamarisks. But the sand up here, unwashed by the short-range tide, was a grubby grey, flecked with tree debris and a couple of stained cigarette butts.

She knelt on the rug. The sand beneath it was compacted into an irregular ridge and furrow formation and however much she tried to smooth out the hillocks and dimples through the woollen surface with heels of her palms, they would not yield. She tried again, this time she lay flat on the blanket and used her weight to wriggle the hard sand into a shape to mould her body.

Once Nick was gently snoring beside her, she gave up trying to get comfortable and went for a walk along the water's edge, manoeuvring round the Sunday afternoon family groups paddling or splashing in the shallows, depending on their age. She felt momentarily sad and lonely, remembering happy seaside outings echoing those of her own childhood; she and Nick building sandcastles for Cally to stamp down with glee before she graduated to decorating them with gardens of flint flats, seaweed and shells, then moving on in her teenage years to the more sophisticated process of damming and diverting streams of fresh water on their way to the sea. Here, in these barely tidal waters, the small pleasures they had enjoyed so much must be unknown to these parents and children dabbling on the shore.

After about half an hour she came back to the rug to find Nick sitting up, pulling on his jumper. A cluster of clouds had obscured the sun, and more were bunching up behind it.

'Have we got anything with us for indigestion?'

'Yes, back at the Relais. I take it you're not feeling too good?'

'It's probably just from lying down so soon after lunch.'

He let out a loud belch. She raised her eyebrows.

They stopped, as planned, at a small grocery shop on the way back. It was open, despite it being Sunday.

'I'll stay here if you don't mind. I'm not feeling good. Could you see if you can find anything in there I could take now. Oh, and a small bottle of water?'

He wound his seat back and shut his eyes.

Looking back at him before entering the store, she thought how old and vulnerable he appeared, and had a vision of how their old age might be if he suffered from some lingering illness and she was required to take charge. She pushed the thought from her mind. Hopefully, they were years away from that, even if Nick was ten years older than her.

She knew there would be no general medication behind the counter. Like mainland France, a pharmacy was the only place to buy that sort of item and pharmacies were never open on a Sunday. She came back with a few bits and pieces for supper, although she suspected she would be the only one eating, and the bottle of water.

Nick insisted that he carry on driving but about two kilometres from Marina du Roc Noir he quickly pulled into a lay-by, opened the car door and swung himself out. His shoulders heaved as his partly-digested lunch left his stomach in violent projectile gushes to land in the border of greenery at the verge of the road. Alice felt relieved that Nick had managed to be sick outside the car rather than in it, then guilt that this, instead of concern for his welfare, had been her first thought.

He remained seated sideways for a while, slumped and hunched over from effort, ensuring there was no more to expel before reaching for the water bottle and thoroughly rinsing his mouth. Alice imagined the sensation of acrid burning he must be feeling in his throat, almost as vividly as if it was her own. He looked pale as he returned to face the steering wheel.

'Poor you.' Alice was genuinely sorry for him. 'Are you sure I shouldn't take over the driving?'

'Actually, I feel much better for that. Must have eaten a dodgy mussel.'

Back in the Relais, he collapsed on to the sofa and was soon asleep.

Alone again for the second time that day, Alice mused about their holiday arrangements in general. Maybe they should try and go away with other couples more often in order to have some company. But that would bring its own set of complications – different ideas of how to spend time and money, Nick's insularity. Of course, he enjoyed some socialising but he preferred it when they were together alone on these trips. He could be at his ease and in benign control at the same time. Alice sighed to herself. Maybe it was simpler this way.

Seated at the table in the sitting room she flipped through a magazine, fiddling with her silver bracelets in between turning the pages. There was a pair of armchairs in the room but she felt unable to relax with Nick's heavy snores resounding from the sofa. She wished he had gone to bed but did not have the heart to wake him and suggest that he move. Anyway, he was such a deep sleeper he would probably nod off again without shifting.

She opened the window to drink in the sound and smell of the sea. It was not warm enough to relax on the terrace with a book; it was too breezy and ribbons of cloud blocked the weak warmth of the sun for long minutes.

'That's what I'll do,' she said aloud knowing from experience her voice wouldn't wake Nick. 'I'll wrap up and go down on to the beach for a bit.' Another hour of light still before sunset and maybe she'd make herself something to eat afterwards. She felt less aimless now she had a plan.

With Nick in the apartment, Alice didn't bother to take the keys with her, a touch of freedom that was long gone in London. On the way out she realised she had been too busy worrying about Nick, when they returned, to notice that the second bedroom was now unoccupied, its door open with the key in the lock in identical fashion to the others. She glanced inside. There was no indication that anyone had been there. The bedding looked untouched, no signs of amateur bed-making, no creases on the pillows. The cheap wicker wastepaper basket was empty. Maybe, she'd been right about the man sleeping standing up!

Outside, she saw what she now expected to see: the bike was gone. Although she was not sorry that the faceless, nameless guest had departed, she experienced a greater sense of isolation now they were alone again. She considered how different it would have been had a couple turned up instead of the biker. A middle-aged pair, married like themselves, friendly, chatty. She would have liked a conversation with the wife, however brief. She laughed at herself. That's probably what was missing, a bit of female company. All the female contact she had had in the past four days was over transactions in shops and a brief conversation with Cally.

Perched on the almost smooth rock she had chosen for the purpose, Alice considered the holiday so far. She wasn't sure how much she was enjoying it.

I must be churlish to think that, she chided herself. Darling Nick has tried so hard to find the trip he believed would suit me perfectly. But then a less kind interpretation of events niggled at the edge of her consciousness – that Nick had paid lip-service to her love of the sea and picked Corsica to indulge his own passion for history and walking. She pushed the notion out of her mind as uncharitable. Even if there was truth in it, she didn't like herself for testing this theory. After all the holiday might be for her, yet it wasn't hers alone.

Still whenever there had been an upturn this week, some pleasure to be had, something conspired to thwart her enjoyment. Or was it she who was pulling herself down? Expecting too much?

Alice knew really that she was lucky to have a holiday, let alone more than one a year, and they'd only had a couple of disasters over the years. This couldn't be classified as a disaster, she reasoned, not like the freezing house in the Dordogne, or the fever she developed that wiped out most of their

India trip, but she could not shift the feeling of depression and disquiet that hung over her here. Maybe, it's me and the menopause, she observed pragmatically. Better make an appointment at the surgery when we get back to London.

She made an effort to shake off the heavy mantle of negative thought. To relish the moment, to appreciate over again the wild beauty of the bay. She watched a cormorant, buoyant on the shifting water beyond the waves' break, then diving for its supper. She waited for it to resurface, counting the seconds it was under and guessing where it would pop up again. She was never right. It bobbed up sometimes nearer her, sometimes further away. It reminded her of those once popular spot-the-ball competitions in the local newspaper of her childhood - the great margin for erroneous speculation. The bird's longest dive lasted thirty-seven seconds, according to her estimation, before it succeed in bringing a fish to the surface, swallowing it head first in three expansive gulps. It shook its head then took off low over the water, with outstretched neck and rapid wing beats, disappearing round the rocky boundary of the bay.

This was the trigger for her to return to the apartment, in a better frame of mind.

The lamp in the passage of empty bedrooms had been turned on, a sign she took of Nick being up and about. She opened the apartment door. In the fading light, she could see a folded piece of notepaper lying on the floor in the hallway. She picked it up, shut the door and, without removing her jacket, examined it in the last of the natural light in the sitting room, where she noticed Nick was still lying prone on the sofa.

It was a short note, written on cheap paper in blue biro. The script was old-fashioned, sloping, bulbous s's and a curly return on the z, definitely the work of a feminine hand. It read: *Sauvez-vous!*

Sauvez-vous, sauvez-vous? She had a transitory image in her head, a French textbook memory from childhood of a woman and child clinging to a life-raft in a choppy sea, a desperate-looking man beyond them leaning over a ship's rail, the speech bubble ballooning from his head spewing out the words, *'Sauvez-vous!'*

Of course, she remembered:'Save yourselves!'

* * *

'Why would anyone do this?'

Alice had woken Nick up and shown him the note.

'I hate the idea that someone, some woman, came sneaking up here, let alone leaving a message like that. Nick, I'm scared. I want to leave this place, now, tonight.'

'Look, love. Consider it logically.' Still groggy with sleep, Nick drew himself up to the task of reassuring her with some weariness. 'This will be the work of some local joker who likes to frighten the tourists. Or a crackpot with a grudge against Bruno, or, most likely of all, some religious nutter who thinks we should seek redemption, you know, out doing their bit on Sunday. I'm certainly not going to react to some local crank and, even if I wanted to, it's nearly dark and right now I'm not physically up to packing up and driving around these tricky roads in the dark trying to find somewhere open this early in the season with room to take us.'

He took her hand, gave it squeeze.

'I'll feel better in the morning, I'm sure. I just need to sleep it off tonight. Tomorrow we can drive further up the Cap as we've been planning. If you still feel unhappy about staying here, we might spot somewhere else we can move to for the last three nights.'

Alice listened and became calmer. She was grateful to him for presenting a reasoned explanation based on bible-bashers, or at worst the resentful behaviour of some small-minded person, rather than telling her she was being ridiculous. The smile she gave him started shakily, then turned to genuine tenderness as a surge of affection for him, for his steady reliability, swept through her.

'Pour yourself a large glass of wine, have something to eat and if I'm up to it, I'll give you a game of cards before bedtime,' he said matching her smile with the warmth of his own.

* * *

Deep sleep, glorious sunlight and the gentler swoosh of a more tranquil sea served to rejuvenate Alice's pleasure in the advantages of their setting. The beauty of the bay, the value of peace from the outside world, the proximity of the sea with no road or vehicles to mar the scenery, the freedom from any regime other than that of their own making, the privacy from other trippers. All these things were stock that once more rose in her appreciation.

As predicted, Nick was back to normal to the relief of both of them. They braved the bottleneck in the village and drove a dozen miles beyond before turning down to a bay, a bigger version of Marina du Roc Noir, far busier, with its own village of serried houses and terraced restaurants threaded with steps and passageways down to a flat beach. The houses were painted serene shades: Dijon mustard walls with pale sage shutters, faded primrose with olive trim; or, nearer to sea level boasting bright white exteriors with lavender, grey, or ocean blue woodwork occasionally offset by window boxes spilling out blooms of salmon pink, scarlet and lemon.

They parked on the edge of the beach, stepping over a concrete lip and an expanse of stone on to sand the colour of milky coffee. Along the tidemark, the sand was overlaid with curving lines of black desiccated weed and small debris, pushed in intense vertical concentrations, reminding Alice of the ink-marks of a heart monitor graph. Further along, the dried out husks of jellyfish caught the breeze, their edges lifting off the sand and dropping back again after each gust.

'Look, it's shaped like a moose,' said Alice, pointing at an inverted driftwood stump slumped on the sand, its foreshortened shape supported by four evenly severed branches, its root crown opening out to resemble the blunt head and muzzle of a moose topped by a suggestion of cervine antlers. At the end of the bay, they followed a path along the coastline crowded with bushes of rock roses flowering in sugar-icing pink and white and stiff gorse studded with yellow blossoms. Dips and rises, twists and turns on the route revealed fresh views of the coast, a stunning mixture of abundant vegetation, rock, foam, sea and sky. Hunger and thirst eventually overcame the exhilaration the vista stirred in them and they wound their way back to the village.

* * *

Alice had no inkling that Nick was on some secret mission. He'd said he was going back to the car to fetch his map and guide book and left her seated at the patio bar halfway up the tumble of colourful houses. She settled into a chunky low sofa, one of several faux wicker furniture arrangements scattered with cushions of acid yellow, pink and lime.

By the time Nick lumbered back up the steps from the beach, the barman had bent down to the table in front of her to unload his circular black tray. He placed two glasses – an ice-filled tumbler for Nick and a flute for Alice - on the surface together with a pottery dish of olives, their green skins dulled by brine.

The barman waited for Nick to fold his long limbs into the low square armchair facing Alice. Then he filled the tumbler with fizzy mineral water and, with a flourish, poured sparkling rosé from a bottle labelled Moscato into the flute. He paused midway to let the bubbles settle, and Alice watched the clear blush liquid fizzle to thick foam in the glassware. The rosé regained its clarity but retained the desired level of effervescence on top. More beads travelled up from the bottom of the flute to collect just below its rim.

'Is special to the island. Made with Muscat,' the man explained before he placed the bill, curled inside a small cylindrical glass, on the table top and withdrew.

The fine mist escaping from the glass tickled Alice's nose pleasantly before she took her first sip.

'Too bad you're on the water,' she said as she replaced her drink on the table.

'Not for long.' Nick reached down the inside of his armchair. 'Look, I've something for you.'

He lay the rectangular package on the table in a gesture of quick detachment that betrayed his mild embarrassment at presenting her with a gift in public, Alice noted. This despite them being the only people in the place, not counting the barman as even he had disappeared.

'Oh, how lovely!' Alice was surprised and touched by Nick's thoughtfulness.

The present was beautifully wrapped in jade tissue tied with thin papery scarlet ribbon, the ends of which, Alice recognised, had been curled into tight ringlets with a sharp scissor blade, a trick she performed at home. A sticker pinned the ribbon to the tissue, marking the gift as purchased from a boutique in St. Florent.

'What have I done to deserve this?'

She turned the present in her hands, to savour its look and delay the moment she would need to despoil the wrapping.

'Well, it's not your actual birthday until Friday when we'll be back home but I decided that you needed a present from Corsica to enjoy now. Aren't you going to open it?'

Alice realised Nick must have bought it yesterday morning in St. Florent. He'd had a coffee and read the paper while she wandered round the shops. He must have done some shopping of his own before she returned to find him.

'I would have given it to you yesterday when we got back to the Relais but events overtook me.' He smiled apologetically.

The ribbon eased off the tissue except where she had to rip it from under the sticker. She opened out the crisp layers to reveal a scarf of fine raw silk, the deep blue of cornflowers.

'Oh, Nick, it's beautiful. And my favourite colour too!'

She held up the scarf to reveal its long, thin shape; turned up the collar of her white shirt and draped it in a relaxed loop around her neck. The ends, cut on the diagonal, hung in soft points which finished midway between her breasts and her waist.

She refused to let the oversized furniture prevent her from leaning towards a grinning Nick and kissing him in gratitude.

* * *

Over a late lunch – pork escalope with wild mushroom sauce for Alice and a plain pasta dish for Nick to aid his recovery – they discussed whether or not they should look for alternate accommodation. They had seen nothing on their journey today but agreed to go and check out a handful of *gîtes* Nick had read about three kilometres further along the road.

They found the spot, which looked promising, so they tapped on a door sporting the familiar forest green Gîtes de France sign. A woman in an apron opened the door, half smiling as if expecting someone in particular. Behind her Alice saw a little girl with glossy brown hair busily occupied with a colouring book and pens. A ginger cat, curled up on an upright chair like the girl, deigned not to look up at the Stennings. When the woman saw they were tourists, her smile faded and she pulled the door to behind her.

Nick spoke with her in French but their exchange was brief. All she could offer them was a one room cabin for that night only.

On the drive back to the Relais they weighed up the effort of driving on to St. Florent to search for a hotel room there, or staying put. The *gîte* experience had rather drained Alice of the willpower to look further. Besides, the beauty of the bay and the space they had in the Relais was preferable to the confines of a hotel room. She said as much to Nick, whose relief at her choice was barely disguised.

* * *

She was naked when they cornered her in the cloakroom of some unfamiliar club or hotel. The curly-haired blonde woman held her shoulders firmly from behind and the other woman, long straight dark hair and an incongruously smiling face approached, arms outstretched to bear-hug Alice with a short bladed knife in each hand. Alice offered no resistance as knives drew whirls, deep enough to pare the flesh but not dangerously deep, in both her buttocks. The perpetrator hissed in her ear, 'You understand things have to happen in a certain order,' and both women disappeared as swiftly as they came, leaving Alice with the reflection of the bloody, symmetrical tracery in the cloakroom mirror behind her.

She was aware of a sharp, stinging pain spreading over the whole area when she woke up in confusion, trying to work out where she was and to shed the frightening image of the bad dream. She became conscious of a strong muscular pain in her bottom and understood it as the nightmare's prompt. She rolled around her side of the bed experimenting with different positions until the sensation wore off.

She pressed her phone. The white digital display glowed 03:25, lighting up the dark. Nick's breathing was steady and quiet. She switched the phone off and set about the task of getting back to sleep again.

She tried her usual formula: eyes shut, slow breath, blank mind to drift into the edge of half-dreamed images, frail like soap bubbles that must be slid into, not questioned by what remained of the conscious mind, or else wakefulness would ensue before oblivion was reached. Alice knew what worked for her but it seemed her body had other plans. She shut her eyes but her mind resisted, projecting a stream of busy pictures in her head, vivid in detail, dark in content, completely unlike the abstract colour flashes she was used to experiencing.

The images marched through her head relentlessly in kaleidoscopic form, coming into sharp focus and then shape-shifting, dispelling into new visions. Green and purple seaweed multiplied in neon explosions. Armies of miniature men trampled over knotted tree roots. The hooded eyes of birds and lizards – beady, black, judgmental – fixed her with malevolent looks before giving way to slithering creepers tacking their way across the ground in a frenzy of speedy growth that instantly transformed them into snakes and giant millipedes. As soon as she opened her eyes they disappeared.

A memory came to Alice of the time that she and Nick had tried a magic mushroom omelette in Thailand, years ago, long before engagement, marriage, or Cally were ever planned. They'd made love for an age that night. Wryly, she recollected their moonlit, drug-enhanced performance. In fact, the moonlight was the only cool thing about it. She recalled how she'd ridden astride Nick on the vast bed, upright, free and shameless, her back arched in passion, her waist-length sun-bleached hair swinging with the motion of their bodies – the sort of unselfconscious act that she'd been too inhibited to perform for as long as she could remember. When did that stop?

On that night, a similar parade of psychedelic images had crawled across her brain for hour after exhausting hour every time she sought sleep. It occurred to her that the wild mushroom sauce she'd eaten earlier might be producing the same effect, in which case she might as well get up, make herself a hot drink and read for a while.

Wrapped in blankets on the sofa, she tried to focus on her book with little success. The repetitive noise of the waves seemed to invade the sitting room, suddenly it was intrusive and irritating, hostile even, playing on her nerves.

Back in bed, she fell into uneasy sleep disturbed by a new nightmare that stayed with her when she woke. This time Alice was the witness of the action, rather than the object of it. She saw a woman, scrabbling towards her along the beach of the bay as fast as she could on that difficult terrain, the long fair hair blowing across her face partially obscuring her features but not her expression, which was one of extreme distress. She looked towards Alice as she floundered, one hand extended to keep her balance. In this hand the woman clutched something blue and dangling, a scarf or shawl; the other held up her long grey skirt as she attempted to run on the unstable rocks. She seemed to be shouting for help but all Alice could hear was the sea. Alice was outside the scene, unable to act and forced to watch with horror as the woman's pursuers, a pack of savage dogs, pulled her down and began to rip at her clothes and body. One dog tugged at her forearm with its teeth. Three or four others swarmed over her. Two of them competed with each other to work at her neck, the bloodstains darkening wide expanses of their fur as they pulled and chewed at their victim. Unable to look away or flee, Alice feared the invisible barrier between her and the dogs would break and when those beasts had finished with the woman their attentions would turn to her.

The feeling intensified when an old and weathered man came up behind the dogs and began to shout commands at them. He was slightly stooped with arms too long for the rest of his physique and she caught a glimpse of bad teeth as he bellowed at the dogs and cracked a whip about them. A howl of pain issued from the animal that caught the brunt of the punishment and the pack stopped to look at their master. He pointed a bony figure at Alice and yelled an order to the dogs.

'Alice, Alice!'

Someone was calling her name. Suddenly she was in Nick's arms, sobbing, while he held her tight repeating, 'It's ok, it's ok. You've had a bad dream, that's all.'

'It all seemed so real,' she said, a little later, after a full account of her night. 'Well, I suppose the first nightmare was surreal, but it was happening to me, and then that poor woman on the beach. It was like watching a film set centuries ago with a hunt much more graphic than any you'd want to watch in the cinema. And then they were coming for me, I just know they were!'

'It must be those dogs and that man up the road playing on your mind.'

She had pointed out the location of the pen when they drove past it yesterday, but the place was too far back from the road to see from a moving car.

'She even had a blue scarf in her hand. Just like mine!'

'That's simple to explain. Auto-suggestion. Yesterday, I gave you that blue scarf. It was imprinted on your mind so it appeared in your dream. We all do that from time to time.'

'Yes, I suppose.' She had to admit that was true.

'I wish I dreamt in colour.' Nick attempted to lighten the mood.

She caught his intention. 'It's more like dreaming in sepia really with some colour, like those early photographs touched up with colour in places. I wish I did dream in black and white, I'd have been spared the blood!'

In the bathroom she studied her naked body in the mirror before taking her shower. A flash recollection, an echo of her first nightmare, made her turn around and look over her shoulder at her backside. The skin, on both cheeks of her bottom was slightly reddened and raised in distinct circular marks.

* * *

The weather was glorious. They decided to spend the day relaxing on the terrace of the Relais, eating a local *tomme de chèvre*, wild boar *pâté* with bread, radishes, fragrant tomatoes and a stubby, knobbled cucumber for lunch. It was idyllic. This is what we came for, thought Alice, her nightmares faded to insignificance and phantoms of the night chased away by the bright, promising day. She realised that the scores on her bottom, so minor that they would now be hard to find, must have been caused by her scratching herself in her sleep.

After lunch, Alice adjusted her lounging chair so her head was shaded by wisps from one of the straggly, would-be tamarisk trees.

She spent the afternoon alternating between reading and looking out over the bay. The sea had lost the disturbing quality of the night and was once again a source of pleasurable fascination, in fact she found it hard to read more than a couple of pages at a time before the compulsion to look again at its terrible beauty overcame her.

The black rocks drew her eye to them, rough and glistening like wet coalfaces after the white foam broke over them, bubbling with the effervescence of champagne and offsetting the pools of turquoise and ice-blue water where the sunlight met the shallows.

The cat was back. It kept its distance, hunched down and turned away from them under one of the breakfast tables. Only the constant backwards and forwards movement of its ears as they flattened and rose to pick up the smallest new sound, betrayed its watchfulness.

Cloud was building up on the skyline, strung out in dense, intensely white cauliflower formations that reached high into the sky and were topped by a smooth anvil shape.

'Cumulonimbus,' said Nick peering over his reading glasses at the advancing inclemency.

'Whatever they're called, they look solid enough to support a great weight of rain.'

'That's what it means, cumulo – heap, nimbo – rain. Heap big rain! It's quite a storm heading this way and we'll have front row seats in the dress circle when it comes,' inclining his head towards the apartment with an expression of boyish glee that Alice found annoying. She would rather there was no storm at all.

As the wind got up, broken dark lines became visible in the water, almost imperceptible at first, then turning into strange ragged-backed mammals that broke the surface and arched back into the deep, a prelude to the white crests that then made an occasional appearance and were quick to multiply.

The wind blew chill. Gradually the cloud darkened to forbidding steel before settling to an unearthly lilac glow. The first rolls of thunder were distant but before long they grew closer, until they sounded to Alice like giants moving oversized pieces of furniture around a room above her head. On the far side of the bay the tower brooded black and bleak in the changed light, its stonework at one with the jet rock cliffs. The air was heavy with unspent rain, its metallic smell reaching Alice's nostrils and pushing away the iodine tang of the sea.

'Best get inside,' said Nick. Alice nodded and started to gather their possessions while he stood staring out over the water.

From the picture window they watched the spectacle unfold, the bright creases of lightning lit up the menacing sky, splitting and dividing down to the horizon. The ghostly impression of their brightness lingered momentarily after the strike, reminding Alice of the aftershock of fireworks.

Then came the rain, first in big, fat drops that left a pattern of erratic sploshes on the window pane, quickly developing into a steady downpour as the cloud, now uniformly grey and misty, swept in.

The next moment Alice's ears were assaulted by an almighty roar. The explosion that followed sent her flying off balance and backwards into Nick. Sparks flew down the chimney, debris tumbled down into the grate and spilled out on to the floor. Smoke welled upwards into the room.

'My God!' shrieked Alice. 'What was that?'

The thunder, following fast on the heels of the lightning bolt, drowned Nick's reply and set the windows rattling in their frames. The property was under attack from elements that seemed set on blowing it apart.

She clutched at Nick.

They both coughed from the smoke and soot.

Even Nick took a moment to catch his breath. But then, as always, he was reassuring and practical.

'Look, it's not bad. Only some bits of broken stone and roof tile. It sounded much worse that it was.'

'Are you sure? What if the chimney's damaged?

Couldn't it fall through? Say the roof is on fire?'

Alice could tell by the look on Nick's face that he had been trying not to alarm her but these thoughts had crossed his mind too.

'I'll take a look from the balcony at the back. I should be able to see if there's any danger. Meanwhile, can you let the smoke out?'

She opened the french doors only to shut them again hastily before they were damaged. Instead Alice fastened the window open at a small angle and left the apartment front door open to create a through draught. She fetched the dustpan and brush from the kitchen cupboard to tackle the mess.

As she crouched to sweep the floor area, another flash of lightning caught the edge of her vision, and lit up the shape of something that had fallen into the grate; the corpse of a long-dead crow. For a fraction of a second, the eye sockets of the bird glowed red.

It was a menacing sight. Alice put a hand to her mouth and screamed and screamed in fright.

As the lightning faded, the eye sockets lost their fearsome glow and became empty holes edged with dried, shrunken membrane.

Nick ran in and turned on the light. Seeing Alice near the bird's desiccated body he swiftly pulled her to her feet and into his arms.

'There, there. It's only a poor dead bird. It's probably been stuck in that chimney since last winter and the lightning's dislodged it.'

Nick stroked and soothed her, his wet hair and forehead dampening her cheek as he pressed against her. She wriggled a little in his embrace, conscious of the moisture seeping into her clothing from his waterproof. He drew back to hold her at arms' length, face full of concern.

'I know, it looks harmless now,' she sobbed. She had calmed down enough to speak, but only if she kept her head turned away from the fireplace. 'But Nick, its eyes turned red, it was so sinister. This is going to sound mad but I feel so scared of this place. It's as though it is trying to frighten us away.'

'Now you are letting your imagination run away with you! You know, there's normally a straightforward explanation for everything. The glowing eyes will just be the odd spark flaring up before going out. You're still in shock from the house being struck by lightning, so I'm not surprised an old dead crow shook you up.'

She looked up into his eyes, sniffed and nodded, glad of his steady reasoning.

'The good news is, the roof isn't on fire and the chimney doesn't look like it's going to collapse. When we're somewhere with signal I'll call Bruno and tell him what's happened. Go and make us a cup of tea and hang up my coat for me, and I'll clear up in here.'

The overhead light started to flicker before opting to alternate between brightening and dimming for a couple of seconds at a time. He turned it off and went to check on Alice. Now over the worst, she was immersed in the practicalities of making tea, heating water in a pan on the stove, assembling mugs, milk, sugar, teaspoons and the cafetiere that also served as an improvised teapot.

'I'd better check the electrics for damage once I've cleared up. The light next door's on the blink.'

He returned a few minutes later to report that the only noticeable damage was a couple of burnt out wall sockets in the living room. He also had a new idea.

'Why don't we give it time for the rain to ease off and then get out of here for a while? How about dinner in St. Florent?'

Alice could not think of a more welcome suggestion.

'Yes, please!'

* * *

They dined in St. Florent's smartest restaurant on its opening night of the season. The setting was spectacular. The outdoor tables were perched just above the sea, overlooking a rocky inlet, and protected from the elements by a sloping roof and side walls with smart roll-down panels of clear plastic. No doubt these would have been secured during the height of the storm but were now raised to make the best of the evening. Nick and Alice shunned the brightly lit interior, hung with stuffed and mounted boars' heads and fishermen's accoutrements, to be closer to nature.

The storm clouds had cleared and a pink and baby blue sky was all that remained of the day. The dark rocks brooded, thought Alice, biding their time, the time when all vestiges of day would be chased away and the darkness would envelop and smother both colour and hope, when all would be like the black rocks. But I really mustn't think like that, she chided herself. She pulled herself back into the moment, the white napery, the gleaming cutlery and glassware, the attentive waiters and Nick, opposite her, rubbing his hands together and smiling in anticipation of his *soup de poisson* with all its attendant trimmings.

As the sky changed to ultra-marine, a wind sprang up, ruffling the water, gradually chilling the Stennings and the other diners. The staff were quick to let down and fasten the thick plastic panes, at once shutting out the too cool air and darkening night, redirecting the focus of the diners, now deprived of the view, on each other.

The dinner, beautifully cooked and presented, was their most expensive meal on the island to date. For Alice, the atmosphere was altered by the enclosure of the veranda, the occasion subsequently downgraded from special to ordinary. As Nick appeared cheerfully oblivious to the change, she kept her observation to herself. She focused on her *pâté* of wild boar with chestnuts, determined not to let on that she would not be sorry tomorrow was the last whole day of the holiday.

They were sharing a *fiadone*, the lightest of cheesecakes made with *brocciu* cheese, eggs and sugar, flavoured with orange and lemon zest and vanilla, when Alice noticed a familiar figure stroll into the restaurant.

'Look, there's Antoine.' Alice waved self-consciously in the direction of the bistrot owner.

She managed to catch his eye just as he veered off in the direction of the bar.

A look of reluctance passed across his face - Alice couldn't mistake it - as he came over to greet them. She regretted her action immediately. Too late to do anything other than act their parts.

'*Bonsoir, Madame, Monsieur*. 'ow is your stay?' And before Alice and Nick could reply he volunteered: 'Is not many tourists in my village so *on ferme le soir*. I come here to see my cousin, *the patron*, but first I visit my sister.'

'Ah, Martina?'

'*Si, si*. Martina.'

Nick shot Alice a warning look as soon as she mentioned the name, enough to say 'don't ask about Bruno', but there was no stopping Antoine.

'I tell her what you tell me. Bruno is back. She say not for nothing would she go back to that house, that bay. Martina, she had strange dreams. She dream about man on tower top, how you say, in olden clothes?'

'Yes,' said Alice. 'If you mean from olden times, from history.'

'*Mais, oui*,' Antoine said impatient with the interruption. Alice could see he was keen to spill out the facts and get to the drink that probably awaited him inside. 'Man on tower, he go *fwwwwarh* into big *coquillage*.' Antoine tipped back his head and mimed blowing into an imaginary instrument.

'Ah! You mean the conch-blower warning people about the pirates! Just like you told me, Nick.' Alice turned to try and include him in the poorly timed conversation. She could feel Nick's resentment that she'd encouraged this intrusion rolling off him like mist creeping over a moor.

But Antoine wasn't done yet. He seemed compelled to spew out all that his sister had told him before he could move on. Alice heard Nick sigh in resignation as Antoine started to talk again but her eyes were on the Corsican, not wanting to miss anything.

'Then she tell me old, old story *notre grand-mère* tell her. You say about pirates, yes, many pirates come to Cap Corse way back. Steal everything. Take men, take women, take children as slaves. A woman, she live in a *petite maison* at Roc Noir. Pirates, they get her. She run away. Chief of pirates is cruel man. He let dogs hunt this woman and kill her.'

Alice heart beat wildly, her hand clenched round the blue scarf, holding down the panic she felt.

'My dream, Nick! Don't you see? It's my dream!'

Nick, furious, rose to his feet, and managed to say with as much restraint as he could muster, 'Antoine, you've upset my wife with your story. I know you didn't mean to but please go now and leave us alone.'

The remaining dinners were beginning to notice that something was amiss at the Stennings' table. A waiter, picking up on the tension, moved forward a pace from his serving station, ready to intervene if need be.

Antoine, nodded his assent to Nick, however, he

had one last thing to say before he retreated to the kitchen. 'Martina, she tell me she dreamed also this story at night before she run from Roc Noir.'

Alice didn't remember Nick asking for the bill, nor did she notice him leave the table in order to pay and get them out of there quicker.

Even Nick couldn't convince her this time of a sound explanation for Antoine's tale. In fact, he didn't try.

On the way back to the car he was tight-lipped in every sense of the word and she didn't know whether to be more scared of what she'd heard from Antoine, or of Nick's dark mood. It's as though he's cross with me, she thought, for making him face the idea that there's something deeply unpleasant about Roc Noir. She fell a couple of paces behind him so he couldn't see the tears that had started to stream down her face.

She wiped her cheeks with the back of her hand before she opened the passenger door so he wouldn't notice she'd been crying. When she took her seat, instead of starting the car Nick turned on his phone, called Bruno's number and thrust the phone at Alice.

'Here, you can tell him about the storm damage.'

'That's ridiculous. I've had no dealings with him and you're the one who speaks French best.'

She cut the call and pushed the phone back at him.

'Why do I have to do everything?' he blustered, bringing a fist down on the steering wheel. 'I've driven you everywhere, suggested where we go every day, comforted you though all these, these fanciful ideas of yours. You'd better pull yourself together and go and see someone – a doctor, a psychiatrist, I don't care who but you're not who you used to be and I'm fed up with it.'

'That's so unfair,' cried Alice. She jumped on the part of his rant that was foremost in her mind, ignoring the rest for the moment. 'They're not fanciful ideas at all! You heard Antoine back there. His sister found the Relais disturbing. She dreamt the same terrible dream as me. In fact, I know most of the reason you're cross with me is because you don't want to believe there's something in what he said, but please don't belittle me or undermine yourself by suggesting my ideas are the product of my imagination!'

'What do you mean?' Nick looked deflated by Alice's attack.

'Well, either you genuinely wanted to reassure me each time I was upset by "my imaginings", or you didn't believe me and just wanted to stop me fussing. And as for all that stuff about you doing everything – you love driving and the point of the holiday was it was a surprise you were organising! Perhaps I have taken a bit of a back seat over the arrangements but I thought some of the ideas you had were things you were particularly keen on doing and I didn't want to stop you.'

The hurt was evident in her voice.

'Alice, Alice,' Nick sighed. 'Look, I'm sorry. I love you and I'm sorry I got so angry just now. Perhaps, the storm and everything that's happened here and Antoine's outpouring tonight has jangled my nerves too.'

The fight went out of Alice. What was the point of continuing to be miserable?

'Ok, I'm sorry too. It's just all been a bit weird. I agree that I am not quite myself at the moment and I will go and see someone when we get home. I love you too.'

She leant across the car to meet his kiss. Afterwards he said apologetically,

'Sorry. Best get this over with before we lose signal,' and pressed redial to try Bruno again.

Silent seconds passed before Alice heard the tinny French female voice. It was a recording.

'That's strange, I'm sure I've got the right number for him but I'm getting the number unobtainable message.'

* * *

The dark, winding road back to the Relais was, thankfully, low on traffic. They drove in tense silence until Alice summoned the courage to tell Nick she was dreading the return to the Relais.

'We can leave tomorrow, if that's what you'd like,' he replied.

Good, she thought, I can get through tonight if I know we are leaving in the morning. Her shoulders relaxed a little and she resolved to reach out to Nick.

'Thank you, darling.'

She put her hand on his leg and he took one hand off the wheel for a moment to squeeze her fingers.

A mouse, or shrew, ran for its life across the road, in front of them. Alice was relieved the creature made it safely to the other side. Further along she pointed out a hunting cat to Nick. The animal's retinas glowed eerily in the car's headlights. It seemed unconcerned by the two dogs, which were busily tearing into dumped rubbish bags nearby, and scattering the contents on the roadside.

Back at the Relais, the living room light shone around the room for a brief second before dying. Nick tested all the bedroom lights which refused to function.

While he searched for a stock of candles and matches, Alice stood with her hands in the pockets of her jacket in the dark living room and looked out towards the tower. She opened one of the french doors and went out on to the balcony. The sea roared in greeting and wind whipped the strands of hair unbound by her ponytail against her cheeks. She was about to retreat inside when she spotted a light by the base of the tower. Its progression was marked by a repeated pattern of twinkling and then dimming almost to extinction, like a hurricane lantern, or torch carried by someone walking about the tower. It disappeared round the back of the tower.

She watched for a minute or two to see if it would re-emerge then called over her shoulder for Nick to come and see.

'There's someone in the tower! Look, there's a faint light coming through the arrow slits.'

'Hmm,' he said arriving behind her. 'You sure

it's not just a trick of the light?'

Alice was riled at his inference. This was not her imagination in overdrive!

'What light? It's dark, Nick! Besides, I just saw some sort of flashlight travelling towards the tower. It must've been carried by whoever is in there now.'

'What would anyone be doing there and at this time of night?'

'How on earth would I know?' Alice snapped back. 'This place gives me the creeps. I can't wait to go home.'

She pushed past him back into the room and stalked off to the darkened bedroom, too annoyed to feel the slightest remorse for taking out her feelings on him.

* * *

She stood gripping both sides of the door frame, the blue scarf clutched in one hand blowing against her knuckles, her bare toes curled over the rough stone edge. The wind blew the long grey dress against her legs and the rush of the waves filled her ears. Alice dared to look down at the alarming drop, down to the black stones and wild sea below her. She knew that she was supposed to jump down to certain death. Something she had done, she could not remember what, had made her deserve this. Blood-borne fear swept through her as she imagined the deadly plunge down to the waiting, sea-washed stones so far below. Their black forms danced dizzily in front of her vision, confusing her sense of equilibrium, beckoning her to join them. Out of nowhere a crow flew at her face, then veered off sideways, startled her, threatening her stability.

She woke up from impending disaster, chilled and shivering in the grey light, to the sound of a horn blowing a single, drawn out lament over a quietened sea.

Beside her, Nick was disturbed from his sleep too.

'Foghorn,' he muttered before rolling away from her.

Alice sat up abruptly.

'It's someone blowing the conch. I know it is.'

She ran from the bed and to the french windows, and there between the battlements of the tower she made out a grey shape. It was the upper torso of a man, arms upraised and elbows bent, his head tilted back, as he blew into a large rounded object.

Hurrrummm.

Pause.

Hurrrummm.

As she watched, the figure and the sound faded away. They melted quickly into the flat grey light, leaving no trace of their existence.

* * *

The sky was still pale when he found her sitting upright, looking out of the living room window, holding herself while she rocked backwards and forwards.

Alice looked up at him, blank-faced, uncomprehending.

'Let's pack up and go now. We can drive to Ajaccio and spend our last night there,' he said.

At the sound of Nick's voice, she snapped back into herself.

'The sooner, the better.'

Now they had agreed to leave, Alice was consumed with manic urgency to be gone. She flung herself from room to room gather possessions, barely stopping to change out of her nightwear and into yesterday's discarded clothes.

She blundered into Nick in the hallway, surprising him before he could conceal the note in his hand. Alice snatched it from him.

The note, penned in the same hand as before, on the same rough paper, crumpled by Nick's hand, contained a simple command: *'Sortez vite!'*

Leave at once.

'Oh Nick! Were you going to show me it?'

'No.' He grabbed the note back from her.

'Back in a minute,' he yelled over his shoulder as he headed out of the apartment at speed.

Instinct told her to run after him – down the passage, down the outside steps, down the driveway and round the corner towards the clutch of houses, where she could see Nick speaking with a woman. He was waving the note in her face.

Alice recognised her at once. It was the shock-haired woman who stared at them that time from her roof terrace, and Nick had apprehended her outside her own house.

Alice approached them. Nick continued to

confront the woman with the scrap of paper, as if leading the prosecution in one of his court cases. His height, his body language was aggressive, but it was clear he was merely frightening the poor woman rather than learning anything from her gestures and mutterings in French, both of which appeared to be employed solely to try to quieten him.

With the same objective, Alice dragged on Nick's arm before he could make more of a scene. She sensed their vulnerability. What would it look like to the other inhabitants who might emerge from their houses any second to learn the source of the disturbance? Two foreigners harassing one of their own? Things could turn nasty.

'*Ssshhh*. Leave her alone. You're doing no good. Please, Nick, let's just get out of here.'

Already, a door had opened above them.

A man's voice called out sharply, 'Saveria! *Viens ici. Maintenant!*'

Alice looked up and saw his stopped figure leaning over the terrace railings. The ugly features that leered down at her belonged to a face that she knew and hadn't wished to see again. The man by the dog pen.

* * *

She tried to forget those awful few moments when their car edged past the houses of Roc Noir. The cold stares of the villagers assembled outside their properties on the roadside, on the terraces above to watch their departure. Then worst of all, when the missile blurred past the sunroof and the windscreen to crash and shatter on the bonnet sending up a spray of earth, pot shards and smashed greenery. She'd screamed out in fright but Nick had kept his cool and accelerated away and up the track to the coast road.

The first hour they drove in silence. Alice twisted her wedding ring round and round on her finger without noticing she was doing so. All her concentration was bent on willing the car to create distance between themselves and the Marina du Roc Noir as quickly as possible. Both Nick and the Citroen obliged her, eating up the kilometres of fast road across the island to Ajaccio.

Alice sighed, letting go of her top line anxiety and agitation. She stopped fiddling with the ring. Now they were away from the place, she was able to think more clearly.

'Nick, what made you run after Saveria back there?'

'Impulse. The likelihood was the note had been shoved under the door just before I found it. So I went outside and saw her hurrying across to her house.'

'Still, that doesn't necessarily prove that Saveria wrote those warnings.'

'That's true, Detective Stenning.'

He aimed a smile in her direction before returning his eyes to the road ahead.

'However, it's too much of a coincidence that she was coming away from the direction of the Relais and there was no-one else around that early. Oh, and, of course, in retrospect I realise she must have had a key to the outer door.'

'What do you think she was warning us about?'

'That we'll never know.'

'Unless it was something that horrible husband of hers was up too. I know! Maybe he was smuggling cigarettes and booze and leaving them locked away in the bottom of the Relais. He might have put Saveria up to writing those notes so he could get at them.'

'And I thought I was the one that reads crime stories!' he laughed.

'Remember I'm the one with the imagination. According to you, anyway!' Alice paused before adding, 'You know, I can't help feeling sorry for Saveria after what Antoine told us about her being married to César Franticelli so young, and his cruelty. It sounds as though Bruno turned out to be a bad lot too.'

'He did have a rotten start in life though. You have to admit, Vanina didn't sound like the easiest of women to rub along with. I believe there's some good in that man struggling to get out.'

Alice remembered Nick had stuck up for Bruno before. She steered the conversation away from the Relais owner.

'I'm sure it was César that threw the plant pot at our car.' She couldn't be sure, of course, because she hadn't seen him do it. 'Shouldn't we report it?'

'What go back to St. Florent? To the police? I don't know what we'd say - we thought someone attacked us with a geranium but we didn't see who.'

'Nick, be serious!' She was immediately cross

with his levity but the point sank in.

He carried on with his theme, 'Should I say that I harangued a local woman and annoyed her husband? I'm not sure they would be very sympathetic. Look, I'm not belittling the situation and we probably should report the damage to the car to avoid an excess fee, but do you really want to spend a chunk of our last whole day in a police station? We've got until late tomorrow afternoon until our flight. Wouldn't you prefer to leave this behind us and enjoy ourselves? I know I would.'

Put like that Alice could only nod in agreement.

III The Aftermath

It was that time of year, dog days in late August, when hard news gave way to image-led stories of animal antics – a captive polar bear sucking fishy ice lollies to keep cool, an arsey swan attacking punters on the Cam, a cat who survived a five hour journey under the bonnet of a car. In-depth advice articles featured topics aimed at women such as ten rules to impose on your newly retired husband, back to school survival tactics. Then there were the daily human tragedies that stuck in the mind, sparking pangs of sympathy for their loved ones from total strangers reading of their ordeals - the body of a father of three missing in Wales, only the canoe had been found; the 10 year old boy and his friend caught in a riptide and drowned; the missing teenage girl who bought ice cream with her best friend a week ago before getting into a stranger's car; the honeymoon wife who fell backwards off a rock to her death, posing for a photograph. The harrowing sight of her smiling face captured by the camera before her fatal slip, stared up at Alice from the printed page spread open in front of her. Look at me, the newly-wed seemed to say, you're alive – enjoy – because I'm not.

She abandoned the newspaper. They needed to eat and Tabbicat was pawing the patio door and mewing to go out into the garden. She was aware of Nick watching her as she moved round the kitchen focused on breakfast tasks. This morning, she'd taken care over her appearance, choosing to wear dove grey linen complemented with silver bracelets and earrings and offset by a scarf that drifted down her dress like purple-red seaweed. Not the blue silk scarf Nick had given her on her birthday. That one lay screwed up and stuffed in the back of a seldom opened drawer. She couldn't bring herself to wear it, not for the time being.

'You look like a beautiful faded child of the sea,' he said, affection warming the tone of his voice.

She knew he'd worried about her during that mixed up holiday in Corsica. He'd told her she'd not seemed her usual self and how he feared it signalled the start of a middle-aged crisis. He didn't say, maybe even some sort of permanent decline, but she reckoned it was on his mind. Only last week he'd confessed that on the last morning at the Relais he thought he might have lost her altogether. The return to their regular routine and a glorious English summer had helped bring her back to her old self. Visiting the lovely new female doctor at the surgery had been helpful too. Cooking for Pomegranates had kept her busy and Cally had come with them for their week in Cornwall, their regular haunt for a few days every year, ever since Cally was six years old. Alice was altogether more relaxed and her sense of humour was in evidence, although she was still a nervous car passenger.

Nick went back to scanning the latest news stories on his tablet, before setting down the Saturday edition of his broadsheet newspaper.

'Good grief, that's our beach, isn't it?' he exclaimed.

'What do you mean?' Alice's first thought had been the stunning expanse of sand on the Cornish coast.

She looked over his shoulder at the zoomed in picture accompanying the news piece. There, filling the whole tablet screen was the familiar seascape of Marina du Roc Noir, probably taken from the terrace of the Relais on a brilliantly sunny day, the stone tower grey and squat in the stark light.

'What's the story?' Her voice fought to keep her voice impassive but inside her head bad memories surfaced, recollections that she would have preferred to stay dormant, forgotten.

'Not a pleasant one, I'm afraid. The body of an English woman's been found on the beach and the circumstances look suspicious.'

'Let me see.' Something about this revelation made her shiver, despite the warmth of the morning.

He touched the screen for her, shrinking down the picture and pulling it back into the surrounding script. Beyond the headline: BRITISH WOMAN FOUND DEAD IN CORSICA and what

Nick had told her there was little detail. No name released yet, said the report, a suspicion of foul play was mentioned and the bay was described as a little known destination on Cap Corse.

A bad feeling ran through Alice, a resonance on the edge of her memory that she could not quite place or connect. She wanted to know more but at the same time she shrank from the idea.

Later, there was a text from Cally. She'd left home early that morning for a breakfast meeting. The clink-clunk of the front door as it shut behind her had woken Alice. The text read:

```
Saw Corsica death on Sky
News. Can't believe it's
where you & Dad stayed.
Speak tonight. Xxx.
```

She imagined the dramatic conversations that Cally might have had about it with her work colleagues. It wouldn't be like her daughter to keep anything so momentous to herself.

She texted back:

```
Yes, such a horrid
coincidence. Supper's at
7.30pm. Xxx.
```

Over the following couple of days the story ran all over the media. Not much more was forthcoming to begin with, just repetition of the initial facts and how the police were carrying out their investigations. Alice was avid for every scrap of information she could find, surfing news channels on TV and online. Then more detail was announced by the Corsican police.

The victim - it was confirmed that the cause of death was neither suicide nor accident – Susanna Grant, 54, from Oxfordshire had been discovered on the beach early in the morning by her distraught doctor husband, Paul. He told police that she had had trouble sleeping since their arrival at the Relais de la Mer a few days beforehand and he awoke to find her missing from the rented apartment. He found her mauled, lifeless body on the beach, her blood-soaked clothing ripped and torn and, a detail that Alice would never forget, a blue scarf still clutched in one of her hands.

She was utterly shaken by the revelation. She clung to Nick, dry-eyed but pleading for comfort.

'Do you realise that could have been me?! It's like my dream! Is this what Saveria was trying to warn us about? What did she know?'

Nick had no answers for her. He shook his head and held her tight.

* * *

More details emerged a week later. Nick found a follow up item in his review of the morning news.

'Alice, you'd better come and see this.'

He had the BBC news page open on his laptop and his newspaper spread wide open on the table to show pages two and three. He pointed at the newsprint.

A picture of the familiar face of Bruno Franticelli accompanied the article, together with photographs of his parents. The pictures caught Alice's attention before the headline. She failed to immediately recognise Saveria Franticelli as the woman who had sensed danger and warned them to go. The photo was so old, the caption was the only clue that the young woman looking sullenly out of the page was Saveria. The other image was of the foul-featured César. She read the article with her heart thumping loudly in her chest:

BRITISH WOMAN MURDERED
CORSICAN ADMITS TO PATRICIDE

Ajaccio, Wednesday, 3rd Sept

A bizarre new twist has emerged in the tale of what now appears to be the deliberate murder of Oxfordshire housewife, Susanna Grant, in a remote part of northern Corsica. Yesterday morning local man Bruno Franticelli, aged 42, turned himself in at St. Florent police station claiming that he had purposely driven his motorbike at his 68 year old father, César Franticelli, knocking him to the ground, and had then ridden over his body repeatedly until he was dead. He has also admitted to administering a fatal poison to his father's dogs.

A spokesman for the Corsican police confirmed that they were about to arrest César Franticelli, in connection with the murder of Susanna Grant at Marina du Roc

Noir last week, after forensic specialists positively identified DNA linking animal hairs and traces of saliva found in the fatal wounds of Mrs. Grant to dogs belonging to the suspect. It is believed that Mrs. Grant was fleeing from the dogs that were deliberately set upon her by César Franticelli, when they overpowered her.

The animals are a local breed known as cursinu, a type of hunting dog. The breed is not normally considered to be aggressive to humans but it is believed that these particular dogs were kept in cruelly confined conditions, beaten and often went unfed. Bruno Franticelli, operator of the Relais de la Mer where Mrs. Grant and her husband Paul were staying, had previously issued a statement denying that his family had any responsibility for Mrs. Grant's death.

Mr. Franticelli senior leaves behind his wife of 33 years, Saveria. In his later years, Mr Franticelli was caretaker of the tower on the shore of the bay, one of nearly seventy remaining Genoese watchtowers that are popular tourist attractions on the northern Corsican peninsular. Stories have been circulating in recent months about his increasingly erratic behaviour and a police complaint was made about him in early June by a pair of German women who claimed he threatened to set his dogs on them.

A former resident of Marina du Roc Noir, Martina Tollinchi, who now lives in nearby St. Florent, told our reporter that she was the cleaner at the Relais for a while, at a time when they were short-staffed. She said: 'It's dreadful news, but in a way it does not surprise me. There was something strange about that place and that old man César was always hanging around. I really needed the money but I couldn't stay on because I didn't feel comfortable there. It gave me nightmares. When Bruno's wife Vanina left him that was the end for me. I left with her. I heard Bruno boarded up the place shortly afterwards and went away. I was surprised when I heard that he'd returned this year.'

She went on to add that the murder uncannily echoes the story passed down through her family of another woman's fate at Marina du Roc Noir centuries ago. It is said that the woman, together with a number of others, was trying to escape captivity from raiding pirates who used dogs to hunt them down. The animals were purported to be full of blood-lust and killed the petrified woman on the beach before the pirate leader could call them off.

Paul Grant, who has remained on the island since the tragedy, issued a statement through police to say that he was 'working through a difficult time and asked for privacy'.

Alice sank into the chair next to Nick's. A range of emotions raced through her mind – shock, disbelief, pity for the Grants. Then she thought about Bruno – how all that rage inside him had boiled over and how he'd sacrificed his future in his anger with his father. Or was it his desire to punish the old man, pay him back for the past? Or to prevent him from harming anyone else? So she'd been right to suspect the bay held some sinister secret, some powerful and mysterious force conjured up from the past to re-enact ghastly deeds in the present.

'Then it wasn't my imagination after all.'

The words came out slowly. She looked at Nick for a response. His mouth moved, half-forming words, as he struggled to find any sort of reply. When he did speak, logic was his master. In terms of reaction, he and Alice were on different pages of the story.

'I can't imagine what it takes to want to kill your own father. All that hatred. And for nothing if the police were already on to César,' he said.

'It's that poor murdered woman and her husband I feel sorry for. And their family. It makes me cold all over thinking it could've been us in their position. Imagine how Cally would cope.'

Alice pleated the sleeve of her white shirt as she spoke.

'I know.' Nick frowned and said, 'Remember the strange biker that turned up for one night? Do you think it could've been Bruno checking up on César? Maybe his father's behaviour was already erratic and he was worried about him, about us?'

Alice replayed the mystery biker's appearance in her mind.

'You could be right, darling. It would certainly explain why the room looked so unused the next day.'

'I'm not quite sure I follow you.' Nick looked puzzled.

'Because if Bruno had slept in the room he could've changed the bedding and made the room ready for any other bookings. Although, wouldn't he have slept downstairs? Surely there would have been a bed tucked away downstairs for use in the busy summer months?'

'Perhaps he felt he was guarding us from harm until he checked out César,' Nick added. 'If César came across to Bruno as being alright, he would have believed it was fine for him to leave again, but Saveria was concerned enough about his mental state to leave us the warning notes.'

* * *

Interest in the story died down as the nation went back to work and back to school after the summer holiday season. The media was gearing up for the main political party conferences, with the result that other news items were pushed out.

Coverage was given to the repatriation of Susanna Grant's body and her heart-wrenching funeral followed in the news a few days later. No more was reported about Bruno beyond being charged with his father's murder. Alice guessed that Nick would go out of his way to enquire about Bruno's fate but not tell her the outcome unless she asked; it would be his way of protecting her.

An odd snippet about the tragedy in Corsica surfaced after the funeral. It was reported that an altar-like structure, a large conch shell as its centrepiece surrounded by a mass of candles, had been discovered when police searched inside the tower at Roc Noir, together with a pile of exercise books. The pages of each were filled with photographic images, cut out and stuck in, from newspaper articles, clothing catalogues and advertisements. The subject of every picture appeared to be the obsession of the tower's caretaker – women.

Her parents were discussing the item over tea when Cally came into the kitchen. Alice offered her a mug of the brew and updated her.

'All those pictures of women, that's *so* creepy, Mum,' said Cally with a shudder. 'I'm glad he's dead and can't hurt anyone else.' She went and put her arms round her mother's shoulder and gave her a hug.

'He must have been a very disturbed man,' Alice replied in a measured tone, patting her daughter's arm. Cally was still her child and the instinct not to be sensational for the sake of it was still strong in Alice.

'Deranged is more like it!' Nick spat out.

'It must've been César skulking round the base of the tower with a torch, or lantern, that last night at Roc Noir! Do you suppose he was going up into it? But how?'

Nick helped her out. 'He'll have kept a ladder hidden thereabouts. There'd be plenty of undergrowth to conceal it. I know we never saw a ladder but we didn't exactly go hunting for one.'

'So apart from sticking pictures of women into scrapbooks what was he doing in there?' asked Cally. 'That whole altar-worship thing is too spooky.'

'Evoking the spirit of the conch-blower it seems,' said Alice. 'I know that sounds potty but I really believe it was the ghost of some past guardian of the tower that I saw and heard on our last morning. Nick, you heard it too, even if you thought it was a foghorn at the time.'

Neither of them contradicted Alice. After all that had happened, anything seemed possible.

* * *

Yes, I am alive, she told herself. I'm the lucky one. It had become Alice's mantra over the weeks since the tragic events on Corsica came to light. All the clichéd sayings about life and happiness now had resonance and meaning to her: count your blessings, live every day like it's your last, you only live once.

One evening in October, when they were alone together, Cally made some remarks that echoed her own thinking. Nick was attending a colleague's retirement do and Alice and Cally had booked themselves a night lounging on the sofa with a Thai take-away and a bottle of white wine. A DVD was queued up ready for when they'd cleared the food away. Alice wore the same brand of plush velvet track pants as Cally, hers were damson coloured, Cally's were black. Both had scraped their hair back into casual ponytails.

'We're doing an interesting piece of work at the moment on women who are fifty plus.' Cally loved her advertising job, despite the frequent long hours.

'Oh? Tell me more.'

Alice topped up their wine glasses from the bottle on table in front of them. Tabbicat uncurled and stretched herself out in luxurious fashion between them, demanding that the dark stripes and swirls of her coat be admired along with her pure white tummy. She yawned displaying the curve of her long white whiskers to best advantage, then splayed out her four white socks to show she didn't have a care in the world.

'Well, I hadn't really thought about it before but there's a lot to getting older. It's been an eye-opener.'

Alice winced in mock horror. 'Go on.'

'It's obvious really. A bit like being a teenager.'

'How so?'

'Well, it's easy to see that thirteen years olds are different in their interests, their likes and their abilities to nineteen year olds but on top of that every year between thirteen and nineteen is different too. Older people are the same but marketeers are constantly guilty of lumping forty to fifty years of life together. Once they hit fifty, all older people are considered the same. It's all about cruises, grey hair and Zimmer frames.'

'Tell me about it,' said Alice with feeling. 'All those mailings I got through the post for stair lifts and alarm buttons after my birthday!'

'We had some women in today representing the different decades from fifty year olds to ninety somethings. I got talking to this amazing jolly lady, in her eighties. Do you know what she said to me? She said: "Enjoy each decade. When you're fifty you wish you were thirty but when you're eighty you'd be glad to be fifty." Makes you think, doesn't it?'

Alice reached for her glass and took a gulp from it to cover her emotions before she could look directly at Cally. 'It certainly does.'

So not only Nick, but now Cally was telling her she needed to get a grip. It shocked her that her daughter felt the need to take her to task, however gently it was done. She was under the impression she'd been doing better, at least until the shocking news of Susanna Grant's fate became known. But then, Cally wasn't to know where Alice's thoughts were heading.

'I think there's a reason you've told me this story.' Let's get it out in the open, was Alice's thought.

Cally's face and neck flushed deep rose instantly.

'Hm, I thought so. Come on, out with it.'

It was Cally's turn to take refuge in a sip of wine. Alice could see her taking a deep breath before explaining.

'Ok, Mum, I can see what Dad means when he says you've changed over the last year but I see it differently from him.'

Alice wasn't sure she liked the hint of conspiratorial analysis about her that appeared to have taken place. She bit her lip and waited for

Cally to say more.

'I think the run up to a big birthday must be a difficult time for any woman. Talking to those women today gave me a better understanding of it, of how it can be different for everybody. I imagine you're saying goodbye to another decade of your life and it's a time of evaluation and assessment but it doesn't have to be a bad thing. It can be a time for starting something new, doing something you've always meant to do, or something that you've never considered possible.' Cally stopped, and pulled a face. 'Listen to me, I sound like some cheesy self-help manual!'

Alice smiled and stroked Tabbicat.

'Actually, you're right, Cally. And this Corsica business has set me thinking about a lot of things. When I think of poor Susanna Grant and her family and how the whole hideous business will affect Bruno and his mother too for the rest of their lives, I know I've so much to be grateful for. With so much sadness and waste of life it's made me feel that it would be sacrilege to take my existence for granted and not make the most of the coming years. I owe it to them, to myself and to you and Dad.'

She picked up her wine glass and took a sip from it before carrying on.

'I've definitely been getting into a rut and it's time for me to make some radical changes. If this tragedy has galvanised me into taking stock, then the next step is to take action,' she said with determination.

'You're not thinking about leaving Dad are

you?' Cally looked frightened.

Alice laughed. 'Nothing that radical! No, your Dad and I are good, but I think what I need is a new challenge, something to focus on and enjoy.'

Cally looked relieved. 'What sort of thing?'

'I'm not sure yet but I've been getting excited thinking of all the possibilities so I must be on the right track. One thought I had was to do less work for Pomegranates and start making my own frozen meal dishes. You know, from home cooking to dinner party stuff but on a small scale. If I like it and it goes well I could pack in Pomegranates. I'd be my own boss, I'd make more money and have more control over when I worked.'

'Oh, Mum, that does sound like a good idea!' Cally's enthusiasm pleased her enormously.

'I think I'll be fifty years young in future, not fifty years old! I might even stop counting years altogether! And, there's more. I've also started making a mental list of all the things I enjoy – days out, places I want to see, friends I'd like to see more of - so I can plan ways of making them happen.'

'That's brilliant, Mum!'

'Yes, it is, isn't it? But right now I'm starving, so let's order our takeaway!'

* * *

Nick got back around ten in the evening. He poured himself a whisky and water, removed his tie, kicked off shoes and joined the two women on the sofa, sitting next to Alice for the last fifteen minutes of the film. Cally had chosen the DVD, a romantic comedy that was climaxing in a wedding scene mix up which promised to end with the right couple getting hitched.

Tabbicat moved from Alice's lap, which she'd occupied for most of the film, and draped herself over one of Nick's thighs. He passed his hand down her back and she trilled and purred with pleasure.

When the credits finished rolling, Cally picked up the remote controls from the table. She flicked off the TV with one and started up some music with the other, a mellow selection she knew they all liked. Alice went to the kitchen to make herb tea for her and Cally and coffee for Nick while the other two caught up on each other's news.

'You know I've been thinking,' began Nick, when Alice had returned with the tray of hot drinks and the block of dark chocolate.

'That sounds dangerous!' Alice teased as they helped themselves from the tray. 'What about?'

'About a holiday. I thought we ought to plan our next one. A winter break, maybe, somewhere hot and sunny.'

Alice paused, tea mug mid-way to her lips, and looked at Nick, then at Cally and back to Nick again.

'Good idea,' she laughed. 'Only this time I'm choosing where we are going!'

A message from the author

If you enjoyed reading THE HOUSE AT ROC NOIR, please would you take a moment to leave a review on Amazon or your favourite book-reading site? I'd really appreciate it. Thank you.

To be the first to hear about new releases, sign up at my website

www.julialaflin.com

I promise not to share your email with anyone else, and I won't clutter your inbox because I will only contact you when a new book or story is out.

Acknowledgements

Thank you, Lane Ashfeldt, for editing and providing helpful pointers, and also thank you to Lizzie Gardiner for the cover design. Caroline Sulzer, *merci beaucoup*. Also, those who deserve thanks for their valuable opinions, kind words and encouragement are, in particular, Moira Lampert and Mary Corran but also Laura Frost, Mirella Gilpin, Jenny Harrison, Kathryn Bonnet, Naomi McCarthy, Clare Cooper-Hammond, Emma Thompson, Harleigh Kehoe, Justine Solomons, Zoe Cunningham, Toby Toller, Ola Olczak and Hugh Toller.

About the author

Julia Laflin has never gone anywhere without a book since reading The Little Red Hen at nursery school. She grew up in Sussex by the sea and now lives in London with her husband, son and two cats and pines for the coast. Julia is half-way through writing a novel which is a family saga set in Greece so watch out for more to come soon.

Julia's non-fiction book credits include:

'Silver - A Practical Guide to Collecting Silver & Identifying Hallmarks' (The Apple Press) - ghost writer and editor.

The New Covent Garden Soup Company's 'Soup & Beyond' (Macmillan) - writer and editor.

Besides working in PR and marketing, Julia also writes feature articles for The Hurlingham Magazine.

Printed in Great Britain
by Amazon.co.uk, Ltd.,
Marston Gate.